Why Me?

Why Me?

ROBERT MULOLO

iUniverse, Inc.
Bloomington

WHY ME?

iUniverse books may be ordered through booksellers or by contacting:

iUniverse
1663 Liberty Drive
Bloomington, IN 47403
www.iuniverse.com
1-800-Authors (1-800-288-4677)

ISBN: 978-1-4759-3773-2 (sc)
ISBN: 978-1-4759-3774-9 (ebk)

Printed in the United States of America

iUniverse rev. date: 10/19/2012

ACKNOWLEDGEMENT

This book would not be possible without you . . .

Blaise Tshibwabwa, you inspired me to get back to following this dream of mine. I appreciate your contribution to the literary world. You've never given up on your side and I congratulate you on all your success cuz.

Karen Simpson, you were very instrumental in the development of this story by reading it and giving me honest and constructive criticism. This story would not be as great if we had not talked all those times. Thank you.

Alejandra Colocho, I will always love you! You, in some way, inspired this story. Had it not been for you, I don't think I would have found any appreciation towards Latin culture. I wish things had been different between us, but God saw it fit that we went our separate ways. I love you and thank you for being in my life. You'll never be forgotten.

Pooja Gulati, Heidi Fortes and Maria Victoria Linares Morales. Pooja and Heidi, you girls are the best. Thank you for proofreading my book. Toya (Victoria), thanks for the translation.

Jeremy Fernie and Amanda Huynh, thank you for the great pictures for the cover page. The two of you were VERY instrumental. I'm looking forward to work on many more projects with you all.

Thank you Naz Zarif for introducing me to them. My brother Eric Mulolo and his girlfriend, Lindsay Espeut. Thank you both for all the support.

My homie for life, Mechelle Waite, thank you for the help on my words. I'm glad you're a part of this chapter in my life.

Last, but not least is the One who really deserves acknowledgement and that is the Most High. God has provided me with this talent. Many times in my life, I made the mistake of blaming God for the bad decisions that I have made, but I must say this here and now . . . I am completely grateful for ALL the experiences I have gone through. I am now stronger than I ever was and I am able to go on in life ready to take on the world. THANK YOU LORD!

Y'all enjoy this book now. It is my greatest accomplishment to date, but not my DEFINITIVE work . . . Stay tuned ;) lol

Robert Modeste Mulolo Beya

PROLOGUE

I'm trying not to get any tears on this page while I'm writing this note. For years, I've thought of writing this. For years, I've thought of the words I would jot down, never coming with something I thought was smart. But for all these years, I've had reasons to keep me from writing it. I've lacked the courage to sit down and share my final thoughts. Now, I've lost all my reasons and I've gained courage from my very good friend that came in the form of this beautiful bottle of tequila . . . PATRON is his name . . . I think . . . Who gives a fuck! I have no choice right now but lay down, drunk and write, before I throw up, of course. One reason was Maria, my big sister . . . She was always full of life . . . I envied her spirit. But now you're gone . . . It don't matter anymore. The other reason was my daughter Shannon, my beautiful child, my gift from God. With her, I felt important, but I also felt needed. I didn't have negative thoughts for a while, thanks to her. She was my rock! You're gone now! You're fucking gone . . . My baby! Everything else was weighing on me too. My mother, although she hasn't been that bad lately, has always been a great source of misery, always belittling me, especially in front of people. Just now she came here shouting and I had to shut my door on her. Why couldn't she say that she loved me? If she can't love me, she can go to hell! Richard's punk ass is gone. You've really hurt me and I will never forgive you for that although some parts of me still remember and miss you. Good thing you're gone! Asshole! You made me lose everything! Punk bitch! Simon . . . I hate you more than anything! You are the MOST evil motherfucker I've ever met! I hate your fucking guts! I hate your fucking girlfriend or wife whoever the fuck she is! I hate you more though! What goes around will motherfucking come back around for your motherfucking ass! Then there's you, Dad . . . Daddy? Father? Mister? What the fuck do I call you when I never even seen you? You a punk for leaving! Christopher's cute . . . He's probably not even interested in me though.

He can go fuck himself too! FUCK EVERYBODY! Then, there's Cooper . . . Cooper . . . I just love writing his name . . . Cooper . . .

I'm going to take the sharp blade next to me now and attempt to separate my wrist . . . There's no reason to keep going . . .

Renee D. Rodriguez

CHAPTER I

October 10, 1998

The convenience store was just quiet and empty that night. Logan Square didn't seem that bad of a neighborhood at that moment and time, much more different than Hermosa.

With a view of California Avenue, behind the store's counter, I spent most of my days looking outside to see the entertainment the streets can offer me; such entertainment would include couples arguing or people performing in front of the store for spare change. I was privy to such treats only when the store was empty, otherwise; I became a watchdog behind the counter sitting on my high wooden stool, looking at the three aisles facing me making sure I didn't have to thrash any wannabe thieves although I had not been consistent with my Muay Thai training.

Closing time was coming slowly that night and I was feeling the torture that the clock was imposing on me by not reaching 11 o'clock fast enough. The sounds of Hector Lavoe's *Aguanile* made the torture bearable.

Plus, I received good news from my teachers earlier that day. Almost two months in and I was already getting praises for work assignments completed.

Even with all the recognition I was getting from the staff at the Wilbur Wright College, I couldn't wait to get started on the remaining projects. I was, however; restrained to keep guard at the store until closing time came.

The clock showed 10:00pm and my situation hadn't changed. I was serving my 5 hour work sentence without parole, looking for an escape, but knowing that I had to serve my time.

I sat there, letting the thoughts in my mind tracing back my steps that brought me to this place.

By the time I graduated high school, Maria had made enough money to move out on her own.

My older half sister, Maria, had dropped out of high school her graduating year. Finding more rewards in hustling men for a living, Maria decided that academics were going against her career plans.

I wanted what Maria had. I wanted to be able to get out of my mother's house and be independent, but I decided to graduate high school. I just refused to go to College, but, unlike Maria, I was not willing to sacrifice my body to be successful in the business she was in or any other types of business the streets were offering me.

Still determined to make money, I answered an ad to work in a convenience store and for two years, I tried to make enough money to get out of the house and get my own place like Maria.

My mother's constant pestering of my situation was my motivation to move out and the cause of my stress. With that added to the low paying job, my patience started to wear thin.

After a while, it became apparent that I was not going to be able to move out with a convenience store job that paid minimum wage unless I worked a 2nd mediocre job or went back to school for a career.

So at the young age of 20 years old, I decided to keep this job and go back to school. I wanted to find a profession where I would not have to worry about. That's how I found myself at the Wilbur Wright College. My goal was to gain enough credits to go to the University of Chicago and enroll in their Law Program.

The gig at the convenience store helped me pay for things like books and other school necessities. The job was somehow still a way for me to keep away from going home and dealing with my mother.

The time was 10:15 when the chimes on the door were heard. Boredom had been interrupted by the arrival of a customer.

The older gentleman limped his almost squared shaped self over to the counter, smile on his face and cane in hand. I reciprocated with a smile of my own. He removed his gentleman guardsman cap, and greeted me with a head nod, the kind of nods that were exchanged by the youths in the street nowadays, which made if funny for an older man like him to do so. His dark skin shade which could've had him mistaken with a shadow would've scared anyone who didn't know him, but I giggled saying, "Mr. Samuels, what brings you here?"

With a voice as deep as James Earl Jones, he answered, "Like you don't know little one."

I laughed. Mr. Samuels was a regular customer who came three times a day: Around 10:00am; 3:00pm; and 10:00pm.

He limped to the aisle and stood in front of the magazine stand, stroking his Magnum P.I. moustache and then after a few seconds, he picked up a fishing magazine.

Looking at Mr. Samuels selecting his groceries amused me. He would always get the same items every day, but he always looked like he was in front of a real dilemma when he walked through the aisles.

As he made his way to the other aisle, he asked, "So, are you back in school yet?"

I answered, as he picked up a bag of pretzels, "Yep! Going straight home to study right after this."

The man, limping back towards the counter, said, "You better! Or you will see my dark side."

I laughed, and asked, taking the exact change from the man's purchase, "You can get darker than that?"

The man stood waggling his finger at me with a smile on his face. After, we shared another laugh; he was out of the store. I never knew my dad, nor was there ever a male figure in my life. Mr. Samuels is the closest thing to a father I ever had, but then again, he was a father that was present when I had my shift at a specific time for 5-10 minutes each time he came.

I went back to keeping company to my boredom waiting for closing time while Big Pun and Joe sang about not being players on the radio.

As 10:30 pm came, my thoughts started plotting. I had to get the hell out of here! I thought that I should just clean now and when closing time would come; I'd be a few minutes early.

I waited a little longer and as I saw that there was no sign of a customer walking in, I just walked into the stock room, in the back of the store, behind the three rows facing the counter, and picked up a bucket and a mop.

When I came out with cleaning supplies, the chimes on the store's front door were heard again and Suavemente by Elvis Crespo started playing through the store's speakers.

I muttered a few curse words under my breath as I hurried to the cashier, leaving the supplies by a wall.

I arrived there and there she was with her almond shaped eyes, just like mine, except that mine were hazelnut colored. She had the same oval face I owned. We could've been mistaken for twins if it was not for me being 6 inches taller, for my skin being a shade darker than her perfect tan or my bigger nose or my fuller lips or my stronger jaw line.

She stood by the door holding a bag. Removing the part of hair covering her face, she lifted up her bag and as perky as can be, she asked me, "What do you have planned for tonight?"

I smiled at her little car salesman tactics and said, "Maria, I already told you last night! I have to get a head start on my projects for school. I am not doing anything else tonight!"

She made her way to me and said, pouting, "Renee, you know we hardly spend time together—"

"Whose fault is it?"

"—I just want to share my spare time with my sister so we can have stories to share with our kids when we grow old together."

I laughed and Maria did the same. Maria never had time for me. She never called and she never visited. She only came when she needed help with something. Most of the time, it was to beat up some girl. I said, "I bet you ain't got no guy to spend money on you, and now that's why you want me to go."

Maria smiled and nodded. I said, "Listen, I would love to go, but you know how mama is always on my back, especially with you moved out. I just wanna do good in school to at least get *her* to cut me some slack."

That was true too. Mama never would approve of me hanging out late at night. She would have a fit.

"Let me ask you a question," as she removed items inside her bag and placed them on the store's counter, Maria asked, "What is your current average in school?"

"School barely started, but I'm close to a perfect average."

With one hand, Maria held up a small red ¾ length sleeve belly shirt and with the other, she held a black pair of tights. She said, "Go in the back room and put these clothes on. I'll deal with mama. Tonight, we have fun, you and I!"

"*Pero Maria . . .*"

She held on to my hand as she cut me off saying, "Not buts, but yours going to get changed."

I picked up the clothes and shouted "*Dios Mio!*"

I started walking towards the stock room, but then realized that I still had to clean up around this place. I turned around and said, "I still have to clean up around here before I go and it's going to be time to close in a few minutes."

Maria said, "I'll take care of it! You go and change now! *Vamos*!"

I obliged her and went into the stockroom to change, seeing that there was nothing else that could be done especially when Maria had an idea in mind. While in there, I turned off the radio and the store remained silent, except for the sound of expensive high heel Donna Karen pumps knocking against the floor.

I took off my baggy blue jeans and my uniform which consisted of a green and blue vest that I worn over my black checkered shirt. After 10 minutes, I finally came out of the closet more uncomfortable than anything. I was surprised to see that the store was already mopped up and the sign on the door was already flipped to CLOSED.

"Maria, I think that this is too small!" I said pointing at my not so concealed cleavage with one hand and covering my exposed belly button with the other. I was not used to dressing that way. I was very self-conscious of my body.

Maria walked over to me and started fixing my clothes, saying, "That's how it's supposed to look. The more cleavage shown, the better the night will be. It would've been better if you had taken off your bra—"

She looked at me and I knew what she was thinking.

"I don't think so!"

Maria put her hands up in the air as a sign of surrender, saying, "—Don't worry about it. We'll work it out."

She then took a step back and looked at me. She came back to me and started fixing up my wavy brown hair, which landed just underneath my shoulder blade saying, "*Estoy tan celoso del pelo*[1]. I wish I was half breed."

---

[1] I'm so jealous of your hair

I laughed, thinking *Yeah right.* Maria then took another step back to see what else needed to be fixed.

"What about this?" I asked pointing at my back side, uncomfortable of the tightness these pants had to my form. It felt and looked like I had nothing on and the thong underwear I was wearing were not helping either, making me more uncomfortable. The thong was a gift from Maria and that day had to be a laundry day of all days.

Maria smacked my ass and said, "It's hot!"

I rubbed my ass feeling and looked at my crazy sister who had just smacked my butt like some drunkard at a club.

Maria smiled and said, "*Usted esta caliente*[2]! We won't work on makeup, since it's going to be dark down there, natural beauty will have to do. Now I cleaned up the floors already, so do what you need to do to finish closing up around here and then, let's jet! Girls get in free before 11:30 and we have twenty minutes to get downtown!"

"Knowing you and your driving skills, you'll get us there in half the time."

"You know it!"

"Are you spending the night at your place or you spending the night at home with us?"

"I said I'll take care of mama, so I will spend the night with y'all at home. Now go ahead and finish closing up so we can go already!" said Maria looking at her watch.

"You smell like Pine Solve and Mr. Clean's love child, by the way."

Maria rushed to her bag and started applying a double dose of Coco Chanel perfume to her person while I walked around the store making sure that the AC was turned off, the backdoor was closed, the cash register was locked and then when everything seemed fine, I turned off the lights and stepped out the little store with Maria, locking the door behind me. I didn't care about cleaning the rest of the place.

I was ready to go, but as I walked towards the car, I was still feeling unsure about the whole idea. Seeing the excitement in Maria's eyes though, made me put my insecurities aside. I would just go along with her. I mean, what could possibly go wrong, right?

---

[2] You're hot

CHAPTER 2

My Addiction

Our little duo reached down to the newest hot spot in Chicago called *My Addiction*. Located on Hubbard Street, this club was making its grand opening that night and many club goers decided to test it out.

Unfortunately for Maria, we arrived a couple minutes after 11:30 which exempted us from getting the free entrance and to make matters worse, we found ourselves in a lineup that stretched around the street corner. Police cars were present probably as a precautionary measure to prevent any disturbance, but no one would stop my sister.

Maria was able to move up in the line with her flirtatious ways. Her sultry voice, the way she flipped her hair or touched men on their arm, the compliments she gave helped us move faster in the line within minutes but once we arrived at the front door of the club, Maria's powers of persuasion couldn't deter the bouncer from completing his task. She had met her match as she found that the over-muscled young man working the door had no interest in people of the opposite sex. So at Maria's discontent, we had to wait for him to let us through the velvet rope.

I just stayed there and did my favorite thing while outside and that was enjoying the Chicago wind. It was called the Windy City for a reason. I just loved the way the windy caressed my face and at times, playfully pushed me. It was a great love affair we shared.

As we stood there, a skinny young man was passing around sheets that had the following message:

MY ADDICTION

Welcome to your addiction. Understand that once you come in, you'll be addicted to either something or someone. Here are your options. Choose wisely:

HIP HOP LEVEL—Old school! New school! PARTY HITS! Free

R&B LEVEL—Old school! New school! For the romantic ones! Free

CARIBBEAN LEVEL—Soca! Calypso! Everything for your whining pleasures! Free

LATIN LEVEL—Salsa! Bachata! MERENGUE! Sultry Latin sounds! Free

DANCE LEVEL—For all of you who love the dance floor! Free

THE ULTIMATE LEVEL—Blends all 5 levels together with an extra twist! $5.00

Come one! Come all! Go to your usual musical addiction or get a new one. Understand that you'll be addicted by the end of the night. Presented to you by Simon "*The Shark*" Smith!!!

Pointing at the flyer, Maria said, "Yo, this is nice! Five different levels to a club. It's crazy! You know where we're going, right?"

"Oh, we are definitely going to the Latin level!"

"Why?"

Giving her a look that said that it was obvious why we should head to that level, I said, "I don't know Maria. Maybe because we are Latinas?"

Maria chuckled a little and said, "First of all, you're only half Latina. Second of all, you are too closed minded. We are not doing the Latin level!"

At times, Maria made it seem as though being half breed was a curse, but always complimented physical aspects it brought, like my hair or my eyes. But I always played it off as though it didn't bother me. I asked, "Where do you wanna go then?"

The bouncer removed the velvet rope, giving us access to the Shangri-La of night clubs.

Maria gave the flyer to me and said as we walked in, "The ultimate level is calling our names!"

As we made our way inside, a battle of sounds could be heard. None were winning. Only the bass had control and you could feel it through the vibrations on the floor.

Two lineups awaited us. A long lineup to a booth was on the left hand side. On top of the booth was the sign **HIP HOP / R&B / CARIBBEAN / LATIN / DANCE LEVELS.** You could tell who was going to attend where as everyone were dressed according to their musical preferences. Some were in baggy jeans and long Tees; others wearing colorful shirts and dress pants; others in tight clothing; some in suits; men and women alike.

On the right hand side was a lineup just as long as the one on the left side. A booth was there as well with a sign that said **THE ULTIMATE LEVEL OF ADDICTION.** Most of the people in that line up was dressed the same, clean shirt, fitted jeans and shoes which were not runners.

Slowly we made our way towards the booth. Maria's mouth started spewing words like a volcanic eruption. She talked and talked about anything and everything. I just kept acting as though I was listening, thinking about school work that had to be submitted. The paper I had to give back about Legal History. The research I . . .

"Renee!"

Startled, I looked around and saw that we had arrived at the booth. A young blonde Caucasian woman was there to greet us in the following manner, "Welcome to My Addiction. It'll be $15 for cover and $5 to come into the Ultimate Level."

I reached into my purse for some money and picked up a $20 bill. I then looked at Maria and asked, "Aren't you going to pay the lady?"

She smiled and said, "I was hoping you could hook me up."

I knew what that meant and I understood why I was part of the trip. I had been played. I put Mr. Jackson back into my purse angry. Maria held on to my arm before I could make two steps towards the door, shouting, "What's the problem?"

Girls behind us started screaming, "Hey! What's taking so long? Move it in front!"

Maria retorted, "Shut the fuck up!"

She then asked me, "What's wrong?"

"That'll be forty dollars altogether that *I*'d have to pay! And that's before we get inside the place! Who's buying the drinks?"

Maria said, "What do you think?"

I looked at my half-sister up and down cause she must be nuts if she thought I was going to spend my hard earned money like that. I scoffed and said walking away, "I'm going home!"

Maria held on to my arm again, but tighter this time and said, "Please don't go! I just want us to have a good time!"

"But you ain't got no money!"

Maria smiled and said, looking at a young man behind her, "Not now, but I might by the end of the night!"

"Bitch, stop talking and move it! We're trying to get in the club!" shouted another irate girl waiting in line.

Waving her middle finger in the air like rock fans would with their lighters, Maria ignored the comment and the barrage of insults that followed. She then looked at me again, putting her hand down and said, "And don't worry. You won't pay anything else after that. I guarantee it!"

I looked and saw the young man Maria made eye contact with. He was looking in her direction with a big smile on his face. She had him and he didn't even know it. I rolled my eyes and said to Maria, "I ain't paying for nothing unless you pay me back by the end of this week."

Maria, waving at the young man, said, "I'll pay you at the end of the night!"

I laughed and made my way back to the booth and paid the young lady the amount of $40 for us. One thing I knew was that when Maria had a guy hooked on her, I got everything that was owed to me paid back in full. It's the nights when she was alone that killed me.

We were then called in by two more security guards, one was female. The man patted me down while the woman did the same to Maria. Maria winked at her while being searched making the young lady blush. We were then directed towards an elevator. We entered with 5 more people that were ahead of us. We felt the elevator move up and listened as the music changed, but the thing that stayed consistent was the bass, in different rhythm. It just gave vibrations.

After 15 seconds, we were inside the *Ultimate Level of My Addiction.* The music was live enough to make anyone want to dance. Even me, who was known to be a stick in the mud, couldn't help but bop my head to the beat. Maria was just letting herself go loose, dancing her way to an empty table with me following her.

The dance floor was a giant circle. About 20 black square tables were around the dance floor separated by a guard rail and each tables had four leather chairs. Bars were at each corner of the room.

Maria and I were amazed as we were not expecting this type of atmosphere. We had literally walked in the Utopia of all clubs. The name addiction suited that club properly. The people seemed like they were in a trance as they lost themselves to the vibe in the club environment. We just started scoping the place looking at the people as soon as we sat down.

We were nonchalant at first, only bobbing our heads to the various sounds blasting out of the speakers. It didn't take 2 minutes before some guy came to the empty chair next to Maria and tried woo her. I couldn't make out what was being said, but I saw my sister giggling and smiling to the man whispering in her ear. Finally he got up, smiling at me and walked off to the bar. The man came back with two rum & cokes and a friend. The drinks were given to us while the friend sat next to me. I looked at Maria interacting with the other guy, in the same manner as she had done earlier. He was very handsome. I took a look at the friend and he was not as good looking, just ok looking.

Both of them Caucasian, the one with Maria was smooth and sensual in his way of talking. I couldn't hear from where I was sitting, but I could tell he was saying all the right things the way his lips curled when he smiled and the way Maria hung on to that conversation, despite the volume of the music surrounding us. His body language showed confidence while his friend seemed goofy and had yet to say anything to me. He just sat there being a spectator to the mating dance between the Alpha male and the Temptress. I looked at him disappointed. I took my drink and looked at the dance floor.

Then, from the corner of my eye, I saw Maria's beau motioning for his friend to engage me. I thought that maybe I'd start getting the same treatment as my sister. Even if it seemed that he was not interested at first. So I straightened up waiting to be wooed. The man moved in closer and shouted, "Hey!"

Nodding with a forced smile, I mouthed, "Hey . . ."

"You come here often?"

Really? The best he could do was *You come here often*?

TONIGHT IS THE CLUB'S GRAND OPENING! was my thought.

I didn't even want to be approached anyway. I looked at Maria who was not paying attention to my not so pleasant situation, so I engaged my suitor. I shouted over the music, "The place just opened today."

"Right!"

The guy looked down in defeat and that was the end of that conversation for me. I went back to looking at the dance floor. In the meantime, the defeated young man assumed that there was no way he could turn his luck around. He shrugged at his friend and walked away. His friend called out to him and then went after him. Maria tried to keep him around, but couldn't as his mind was already made.

As he walked away, Maria looked at me, with an angry look. From across the table, she shouted, "Stupida! That was our drinks that you managed to chase out of here! Try to be cool!"

Why didn't she ask me what happened? Why did I have to be stupid? I didn't want to be hearing any more insults coming my way. I guessed that I had to be nicer with the next one.

Another gentleman came along to talk to Maria, by himself, with a drink offering for me and her, but this time, Maria chased him away as he lacked the smoothness the previous guy possessed. And it was the same pattern for all the other guys that came after him: Approach, drinks, rejection. It gave us some laughs and allowed for us to loosen up.

Like little girls, we were giggling and laughing at everyone walking around the club, making fun of the way they danced or the way they were dressed. And if we were not making fun of people, like judges at a competition, we would look for the best looking man in the place, Maria imagining how big certain body parts were and me laughing at her comments. The only disadvantage was that we could only communicate by shouting at one another to understand what we had to say to each other.

After a good 45 minutes of mocking others, a man in a dark suit sat right next to me. Being picked over Maria surprised me because it never happened. He wore a navy blue double breasted suit with a black tie and a black dress shirt underneath. The fact that he was dark skinned himself didn't help the situation. But there was ONE distinctive attribute to him . . . his smile. A grin so wide on a face so round, it almost made him look like The Joker from the movie Batman. Nonetheless, he remained handsome, even in the darkness.

The young man extended his hand towards me, leaned over and screamed out, "Hi, my name is Simon. A lot of folks call me Shark!"

I shook his hand and replied screaming, "Hi, my name is Renee!"

Pointing at Maria, I said, "That's my sister, Maria!"

Simon waved hello to Maria and she did the same, looking attentively at the development of my situation.

Simon leaned over again and screamed out, "I own this place and I don't like the fact that you guys are seated here! Why don't you come to the VIP? It's not as crowded as this area, the music is not so loud and all the drinks will be on me!"

He pointed at a section above the club. The section was only reachable by stairs guarded by two bulky gentlemen in black suits. The VIP section was a room with a giant glass window overlooking the dance floor, but really made out for the people on the dance floor to be envious of those who were enjoying themselves inside the VIP section.

Simon had this demeanor that exuberated confidence, bordering cockiness. Almost as if he didn't know what a rejection looked like. However, I was not born yesterday. How many guys dressed in suits could come up to me saying that they were the owner of this place? I refused to be played.

I gave an insincere smile and screamed out, "Thanks, but no thanks! We won't be staying here too long anyway! Plus I don't think my . . . I mean, our boyfriends would not approve!"

The Shark unshaken by the answer smiled and screamed out to both of us, "From now on, all your drinks are on me . . ." He then smiled and said in my ear, ". . . even your boyfriends!"

He rolled his eyes after saying that. He pointed at the VIP and continued, "If you're looking for me, I'll be over by the VIP overlooking this spot where you girls are at!"

Simon then looked over at the bar and made a few hand gestures. He then got up, shook hands with Maria, flashed a big smile for me again, and then left, as cocky as he came.

After Simon was at a safe distance away from us, Maria got up from her seat and quickly sat next to me. She then asked, screaming, "What was that about? Who was this guy?"

I screamed back, answering, "That was just some guy saying that he was the owner of this place!"

"What was his name?"

I started laughing and screamed out, "His name is Simon!"

Maria's eyes widened as she asked, "Did he have a nickname?"

Surprised, I said, "Yeah! It's Shark! How did you know he had a nickname?"

Maria's eyes opened wider, "What did you tell him?"

"I told him that we were not going to be staying here too long and that our boyfriends wouldn't appreciate if we hung out with him!"

Maria shouted, "*Estúpida*! Do you know what you just did to us right now? You just took away our drinks for the night, AGAIN! The Shark is the owner of this club!"

"What makes you think that he is the actual owner? He could be putting up a front!"

A staff member from the club then arrived at our table with two drinks on a tray. As he placed both drinks in front of us, he said, "The Shark just advised me to take care of your orders and give you as many drinks as you wished."

Maria asked, "Who's paying for this?"

The young man pointed towards the VIP and said, "It's on The Shark's tab!"

I looked over at the VIP and there was Simon, looking straight at me with a big smile. With his hand, he made a gesture to invite us one more time at the VIP. I kept looking. He then put both hands together, as though he was praying and mouthed please with his mouth. That made me smile, and so I nodded. I turned to Maria and said, "He's inviting us to the VIP! Wanna go?"

Maria picked up her bag, took my hand and dragged me to the VIP section.

Once we walked in, bottles were already on tables. Three men were seated on a long leather couch enjoying the drinks while two women were dancing with each other. They were dressed more like they were heading to an executive meeting instead of your regular club attire. In that section of the club, the music was not that loud. You were able to talk without having to yell at one another.

The lighting in the VIP room was much better and we were capable of getting a better physical overview of the Shark.

"Welcome to the VIP," said Simon without having to yell. He then asked, "Will your boyfriends be joining us?"

I smiled and said, "I didn't believe you were who you said you were, so I lied."

Simon flashed that big smile of his again. Maria then extended her hand towards him and yelled out, "Hey! How you doing? I'm Maria, Renee's sister!"

Simon smiled and said as he shook her hand, "Yeah, she had told me earlier. I'll make an assumption and say that the two of you ain't got the same father or mother, am I right?"

"Good eye!" said Maria, "You see, my eyes are just as good, so since I can see that you are interested in my sister and not me (crazy), could you introduce me to some of your male friends here, just so I can go to work here and leave you guys to get better acquainted!"

Simon let out a big laugh and said, "I like you! Straight to the point! Well, you know what? You can go ahead and introduce yourself to them. They won't bite you!"

"That's too bad!" said Maria, turning to the rest of the party, "I was hoping they would!"

She was making her way towards the other people sharing the VIP room, but then stopped in her tracks and looked at Simon and said, "Don't get any ideas with this one. She will whoop your ass!"

Maria then walked towards the other patrons of the VIP section. I shook my head, feeling a little embarrassed by her comments. I then felt my hand being held. It was the Shark trying to lead me into a corner of the room. Simon made a head motion for me to follow him. There, a table with two chairs could be found, but I stood where I was and shook my head no. Fear of the possibility of being in the presence of a maniac took me over. I didn't come for this. I came for Maria.

Maria reappeared and asked Simon, "Where's the bathroom?"

He pointed at a door that was at the backside of the room. Maria said, "Thank you!"

She then dragged me towards that door. As we entered the bathroom, Maria asked, "What's wrong with you?"

"What do you mean?"

"The man was nice enough to invite us in here without making us pay and you're going to act all stupid now?"

There was that word again. Whether in English or Spanish, the word stung. "Stop calling me stupid, Maria! He's trying to isolate me! I'm not down with that!"

Maria sighed loudly, looked at the floor, tapping her foot impatiently, and then looked at me again. She then asked, "Do—"

"Don't! Do not call me that!"

"Fine," said Maria, "Tell me one thing then . . . Did you ever get asked to go in a corner by some guy before?"

"No, it has never happened."

"What do you think happens in a corner like that? When I'm in the same room and I have my eye on you at all time? Do . . ."

"Don't call me that! Or I will go home!"

Maria took a deep breath and said slowly, "He wants to get to know you and in order to do that, he has to talk to you."

"I don't know Maria. I'm just not used to getting that much attention from a guy."

Maria shouted, "Do you know why you never get asked out? Because you're not accessible and I don't mean for sex! I mean that you keep your guard up no matter what! Where do you get that? Understand that in life, you either take chances or you lose out on opportunities!"

I looked at Maria, knowing that she was not saying that only because she wanted to have a good time. A lot of truth was being said in that little bathroom. Guilt took over me. Talking to some guy would not be the end of the world. I hugged Maria and said, "Thank you! But promise me you're going to have my back if anything goes down."

"Don't worry and have fun, *querida*! If you don't want to fool around with him, then don't, but make sure you have fun!"

I looked at Maria and started feeling a little scared. That meant that I had to get out of my comfort zone. There was a reason why they called it "comfort" zone. I wanted to make my sister happy, so it was probably worth being uncomfortable for a couple of hours.

I closed my eyes, took a deep breath and imagined that if I was Dorothy from the Wizard Of Oz, I might be able to click my heels three times and reach home, but I knew better. I opened my eyes and said, "Let's go have fun!"

Maria raised her fist in the air and yelled out, "Let's go!"

So we walked back in the VIP room. Simon was at the corner by himself with a bottle of Grey Goose and a bottle of cranberry juice, looking out the big glass onto the dance floor. I went and sat right by him. Simon asked, "Is everything all right?"

"Yes, don't worry about it."

"Good to hear. For a minute, I thought that I offended you or something," said the Shark as he started pouring the drinks in the glasses. "Was your sister playing when she said you'd kick my ass?"

"Well, I had more enemies than friends in high school, so I had to learn to defend myself. Come to think of it, I don't think I had a friend besides . . ."

I had to think about that one. So much pain. I snapped out of it when Simon said, "You were saying?"

"Oh! Yes! Maria was my friend. My only friend . . ."

Uttering those words pained me. I continued, "So I had to learn how to defend myself."

"Damn!" responded Simon, "The boyfriends didn't mess with you too tough did they?"

"I was not too popular with the boyfriends either," I said, with a forced smile.

Simon asked, "Were the guys blind in your school?"

I tried to hold a smile. I don't get that many compliments, so when I get them, I usually smile from ear to ear. I didn't want to. Simon, smiling proudly, asked, "Why you trying to stop yourself from smiling there?"

"Cause that was cheesy!"

Simon laughed and said, "Cheesy, but you liked it!"

I laughed and said, "Whatever!"

He took a sip out of his drink and said, "So, what's your hustle?"

"My hustle?" I asked almost laughing.

"Your hustle! What do you do for a living?"

"I know what it means! It's just that I wouldn't expect YOU to talk like that."

"What do you mean; you wouldn't expect ME to talk like that?"

"You're a suit. You look a little too bougie to talk like that."

Simon laughed and then said, "Appearances can be deceiving. I was raised in West Philly, which is not a bougie town if you get what I mean. I was lucky enough to get into this type of business."

I took a sip of my drink and said, "I see."

"You still *ain't* told me what you do."

I smiled and said, "Well I work in a convenience store in Logan Square, part time, but I am a full time student at Wilbur Wright College."

And our conversation continued there. I told him about my aspirations to become a lawyer and how I wanted to pass the bar in 10 years. I even told him that the person who inspired to be like that was Claire Huxtable, saying that she was black, speaking Spanish and a lawyer and a great mother. Something that I wanted for myself.

He told me the reason why he was being called Shark was due to his humongous smile, but I didn't believe him.

Little by little, my insecurities and fears were becoming non factors as I answered more of his questions and as he created more questions for me to ask.

A good hour had passed as rapport and a sense of familiarity started building between the two of us. Cohesiveness was almost being formed, when the song *No No No* by Destiny's Child came on. I closed my eyes, put both my hands in the air and screamed out, "Ooooh! That's my song! That's my song!"

It was my song. I was in front of my full length mirror singing and dancing that song and others every night.

The Shark smiled and said, "Well, my dear, how about we go and dance now?"

I looked at him and was about to turn back to my sheltered ways, but then caught a glimpse of Maria. She was smiling with her thumb up. I remembered our talks in the washroom and thought that I didn't want to be a Debbie Downer, plus I was enjoying Simon's company. So I took his hand and started to dance with him, right there in the middle of the VIP room. I had both my hands on his shoulders and he had his hands on my back, two stepping. As we danced, I sang the lyrics to the song smiling, as if I was at prom; prom that I missed. The song ended and the DJ played *Rappers Delight* by Sugarhill Gang. I was about to go back to the table, but Simon held my hand and said, "Come on now! We already up, let's have some fun and dance some more!"

"I don't know. I'm not too hip hop."

"Ok, but it's my song!"

I laughed because I knew that it was not his song. I looked at him trying to provide a little rocking of his hips still two stepping. I decided to show him how it was done, like I knew how. So I raised my hands in the air and moved his way concentrating on my movements, hoping that it looked ok; moving my hips to the left and the right and then the left again and then the right again. I was starting to get into a rhythm. I had not noticed that the DJ was mixing tracks in between, but I was still dancing concentrating on my moves.

If I had paid attention, I would've noticed songs like *Dangerous* By Busta Rhymes; *Too Close* By Next; *Make Em' Say Uhh!* By Master P; *Touch It* By Monifah; and *Getting Jiggy Wit It* By Will Smith.

All I did was following the beat and then, as the beat slowed down, I noticed Simon had been behind me the whole time. He had been sweating and I think I was the cause. He took both my hands and placed them on his shoulders. We danced on *Weak* by SWV.

I had so much fun dancing that I had totally forgot that I was in the club dancing like I was. I was just enjoying myself.

Simon said, "You know that I'm having a really good time with you right?"

"I'm enjoying myself too."

Being so close to the man, I realized that he was at the very same height as me.

"You'd like to come with me after this?" Simon asked.

Right there and then, my sense of insecurity came back full force. Maria said there wouldn't be sex and I didn't want to. He was getting ideas. I backed away and said, "Sorry, but I really don't want you to think that we'll do anything just cause of a few dances that we had! I ain't that type of girl and I don't want you to think that of me either! And also . . ."

"Chill, Renee! Chill!" said Simon, with a smile on his face, pulling me back towards him, "I was just asking! I'm glad you're saying no. To me, that means that you're not one of them chicken heads that wants to get with me for an opportunity to hang out in my club for free. I wanna see you again though."

"What do you mean?"

"Well . . . I really like you. I want to take you out to dinner sometime. I want to get to know more of the future Mrs. Huxtable. So tell me . . . What do you say?"

I looked at him, not knowing what to answer. The last time that I had been asked out, was quite a while ago and things had not turned out nice either, but what wrong could've come through from this?

"I'd like that."

Simon flashed his big sharky smile and said, as he handed me a card, "I want you to keep my number. I want you to be totally comfortable with me; therefore, I want YOU to call me so we can set up a time when YOU'RE ready to go out."

I took the card and smiled saying, "Thank you."

I then remembered Maria. I looked around and saw that she was pretty much a goner right now, on a couch, passed out, with a guy next to her who as well was passed out with his hand inside her shirt.

I said, "She was supposed to be my ride."

The shark looked at my intoxicated sister and said, "Don't worry. I'll have a limousine drop you guys home."

I asked, "What about her car?"

Simon took a moment to think. He then said, "I can drive you guys to your place if you want."

I looked at him, wondering if I could trust him. Recognizing the look on my face, Simon said, "Listen, I can't fight for shit, so if anything goes down, you'll probably whoop my ass, just like your sister said. You can be in the backseat with your sister. I'll be the taxi man for you guys tonight."

I was still perplexed. Getting some strange guy to drive me and my sister around, but then again, what option did I have? I was not going to drive her car. I didn't even have my permit yet. Simon then said, "You either take this offer or you go with my limo to your place and leave your car in the parking lot. You tell me which one you want."

I was no thug, but I knew the streets of this city and what people were capable of doing in the middle of the night. I then said, "You'll drive us home, but no funny business!"

Simon once again smiled. He said, "I have to go and make sure that everything is settling down properly before the spot closes, but afterwards, I'll drive you guys home."

I nodded and Simon went downstairs. I made my way back to the couch and as I sat next to Maria, I removed the gentleman's hand from her shirt, which in turn woke him up. He looked around and asked, with a slurry accent, "Where's everyone?"

"They've gone home."

He said, "Oh ok."

He then passed out.

It took about 45 minutes for Simon to get back. When he did, I asked, "What's going to happen to this guy?"

Simon looked at him and then said, "We'll have a taxi called for him. We should get going now. The club has been cleared out and we can move and get your sister's car now."

He then went to pick up Maria in his arms and we walked out of the club together. I was enjoying this feeling, being out of my shell. I allowed myself to live a little without thinking of the consequences and I came out without a scratch.

We arrived in the parking lot and it was empty except for a few cars which most likely were left behind by people who were too drunk to drive.

Simon asked, "Where's your car?"

I pointed at the dark blue '87 Corsica. Simon looked at the vehicle and then back at me. I couldn't help but smile because he probably never been in a mediocre vehicle like that one being a club owner and all. He said, "Y'all gots to be kidding me . . . You're afraid that people will steal this car?"

"You really don't know this city, do you?"

I took the keys from Maria's purse, stuck them in the door and then turned them. I then took a step back. Simon perplexed asked, "Aren't you going to open it?"

I said, "Wait a minute!"

I then kicked the driver door and all 4 doors flung open. Simon said, "Oh my goodness! You guys are GHETTO!"

I said, "Not me! It's her car . . . I'm just used to seeing her doing it."

Simon laughed as he laid Maria in the backseat. Then as he saw me making my way towards the front of the car, he asked, "Aren't you going to sit with your sister?"

I looked at the backseat and said, "She ain't going nowhere."

I smiled as I saw Simon smiling. I was feeling more comfortable with this man. I don't know why, but I was.

CHAPTER 3

Reality

"Is this the time a young lady comes home to her mother's house?"

Esperanza Conchita Rodriguez, my mother, a little heavyset brunette with a few grey hairs on her head, was standing at the bottom of the stairs wearing a pink night gown.

Her strong Spanish accent only accentuated the anger in her voice. She probably was expecting me to walk in by myself, but seeing Simon behind me holding Maria in his arms must have sent her over the moon. She just stood there, with the favorite outfit her face liked to wear; her glasses and a scowl.

I closed the door and said, "I'm sorry mama. Maria wanted for the both of us to go out tonight and she got a little carried away."

Mama said, with her arms crossed, "Don't try to blame your sister. You have responsibilities Dolores! You're in school and your sister is not! You have midterms, she doesn't! Her life is made and you're about to mess up yours cause you're too stupid to know better!"

There was that word again. That word stung worse coming from mama than it did from Maria. Mama then looked at Simon with a cut eye look and looked back at me and said, "So you brought this man here to have sex in my house? I'm sorry but you're going to have to be a *puta* outside of here if that's the case Dolores!"

Simon started, "Oh actually, ma'am, that's not the case! I'm just . . ."

Mama cut him off and said, "Excuse me, Mr. Man! I don't care what you have to say! This is between me and my daughter!"

I said, "Mama, he is just the owner of the place we were at. He helped bringing Maria's car back."

"Use whatever excuse you want! You can't fool me! I know a *puta* when I see one! My husband used to be a police officer after all! I can recognize these things. Look at how you're dressed."

I looked at my clothing and forgot that Maria had given me those God awful clothes. I probably would've had the same impression if the shoe was on the other foot, but then again, I'm sure that even if I came in dressed like a nun with the Pope, mama would've assumed that I corrupted the Holy Father into fornicating with me.

I started, "But mama . . ."

She shouted, "*Usted me repugna*[3]*!*"

Really? I repulsed her? She walked away without looking back at the damage she caused. She just left me there with Simon and Maria in his arms. I was humiliated. He probably didn't understand the Spanish, but that didn't take away the pain that was caused just now.

I fought them. I swear I did. But they were warm and just wouldn't obey as they flowed down my cheeks. I didn't want to cry aloud, but whimpers were heard. Always, Mama had to do this to me and leave me like that. Maria could never do wrong. She was the perfect child. I was the demon baby. She didn't even come back down, which showed she had no remorse.

In an attempt to lighten the mood, Simon said, "Your mom is not so easy to handle, now is she?"

I didn't even respond. The pain and humiliation was too great. Not that it was the first time my mother attacked me like this, but it was never something that I allowed myself to get used to. Simon asked, "Where do you want me to put your sister?"

Still whimpering, I responded, "In the living room."

Simon walked towards the living room and dropped Maria on a couch there. He then came back to the lobby where I was still standing looking at the ground. He took me in his arms and I let everything out, crying, not only because of the pain of the words, but also because I felt like I played myself. I came out of the club forgetting that I had another life that was waiting for me and that I had to be coming back to this bullshit reality. Simon asked, "Where's your kitchen?"

---

[3] You repulse me

Still crying, I walked towards the dark empty kitchen. Following me, Simon asked, "Can you get 2 glasses?"

I got them out and sat at the dining table. Simon opened the fridge door and then took the milk. He then filled the glasses and put them both in the microwave and punched in 1 minute on the appliance. Simon took out the glasses of milk as he heard the microwave beeping and then sat with me saying, "When my father started messing with me when I was a kid, my mom would get me a hot glass of milk for me to drink and just talk to me to make me feel better."

I wiped my tears, took a sip from my hot milk and said, "I'm so sorry you had to see this! It's not the impression that I wanted to give to you."

Simon put his hand on my face and said, "Don't worry about it. Are you ok though?"

I looked at him as he touched my face. It had been long since I allowed a man that close to me, but I needed the attention. I needed to have someone who cared.

Yet I still felt like I had to send him on his way home. So I took his hand from my face, held it in both my hands and laid it on the table saying, "Thanks for being so considerate Simon. How do you plan on going back home?"

Simon smiled and said, "I'll be out of here soon. Will you be cool?"

I smiled and said, "Thank you."

"Can I ask you a question?"

"Sure." I said sniffling and taking another sip of milk.

"Who's Dolores?"

I covered my mouth with my hands to prevent the milk from spewing out as I almost let out a big laugh. I forgot that he was not aware of the way things worked around here. Removing my hands, I gulped whatever milk was left in my mouth and said, "It's my middle name. My mother only calls Dolores."

"She don't like Renee?"

"The man who's supposed to be my father called me Renee. Apparently, he was there at my birth, but after an argument between him and my mother, he decided to leave. She never heard from him after."

"Sad to hear," said Simon. A ringing sound was heard, but it was not the house phone. He pulled out one of those new cellular phones out of his inside pocket and answered. He talked for a bit and finished by saying, "I'll be right out."

He turned to me and said, "I have to leave now."

Simon got up and made his way towards the front door, with me right behind him. I liked his company and all it took was a little night out. Come to think of it, I really don't regret meeting him. The night ended badly, but I was happy that I met him.

I walked outside the door with him and stood on the porch. He asked, "So you got my number . . ."

I smiled and said, "Yes, I do."

"You're planning on calling me?"

As I saw the limousine pull up in front of the house, I said, "You'll see,"

Simon turned again to face me, but I was already inside the house with the door halfway opened, my head sticking out. I said, "Thanks again, Simon. You have a good night."

Simon smiled and said, "I'll talk to you later . . . Hopefully."

I returned his smile and then closed the door.

I then stood in the entrance, smiling, taking in the last few moments that I spent with Simon. If only every time mama came after me, it could end like this, I would be . . .

My moment was interrupted as I heard Maria make a horrible sound in the living room. I knew what that meant. So I went in the kitchen, picked up a bucket and a mop and went in the living room. Maria had regurgitated whatever she had ate that day on the couch and on the floor. I went in and started cleaning, as though I had been trained to do so. I scrubbed with the mop as hard as possible. Many times, I was tempted to shove it in Maria's opened mouth as I heard her snore away.

I'll deal with mama. Don't worry about mama. Who's stupid now?

Once done, I heard my mother, "Look at you! Just good for nothing!"

I turned and saw her standing there behind me. I looked up as though she wanted to kick me. And here I thought the night was done.

"Mama, why are you on my back tonight?"

"You bring your men here and your sister is in this poor condition. If I hadn't stayed up and caught you, you would've probably just have gone for your sex with that *Negro* while your sister is here suffering!"

"Mama, for the last time, he helped us bring Maria's car from the club! *Tu no no comprendes*[4]! It was all Maria's idea to go! Why do you think the worst of me?"

"Cause you never proved me wrong!"

My mother took one last look at me and then went back upstairs, disgusted by what she saw. I watched her leave and MY anger started to rise. I had done nothing wrong and she was putting all the blame on me. That was too much.

I took the bucket and the mop and threw them inside a closet, hoping to make as much noise as possible. I then stomped my feet up the stairs, making more noise, the same way a 5 year old would. I finally slammed the door of my bedroom behind me. My window was opened, so the wind helped in slamming the door extra loud.

I picked up the covers from my bed and my pillow and threw them on the ground and then cried myself to sleep, hoping that a change would come because I was tired! I was tired of coming home to this every day!

The next day, I woke up to the sounds of Puff Daddy's *My Señorita* and light kicks of a hung-over Maria who stumbled into my room with 2 cups of coffee in her hands. Slowly remembering the night before, the pain came along with the memories. Maria sat down at the edge of my bed. She asked in a groggy accent, "What happened last night?"

I took the pillow I was sleeping on and threw it at her. After the pillow made contact with her head, Maria winced and then took a sip of her coffee. She then said, "Let me guess . . . Mama again?"

I got up and felt the wind caressing my face again, as to say good morning. I lightly smiled and then began changing into a grey jogging pants and white T-shirt as if Maria was not present. Putting my hair in a ponytail, I said, "You said that you'd handle her last night!"

Maria said, "*¡Lo siento!* I brought you some coffee though."

I started stretching my arms, legs and neck. I then sat on the ground and started doing sit ups for a couple of minutes. Going back to my training, I started throwing punches and kicks as Maria looked on. I loved shadowboxing, especially after I was upset.

I was rusty. I did not exercise as much as I did when I first started training, but last night required that I let out some steam or I was going

[4] You don't understand

to be a total bitch to Maria and the rest of the world and that would not be a pretty sight.

Every time I did that, I remembered how it all started. I remembered what forced me to learn how to fight. I remembered because I promised myself that I would never forget.

CHAPTER 4

The Wolfpack

"Pick that shit up, Mulatto!"

I was at my locker, 15 years old, looking at the mess created by Jessica. Miss popularity. She wore clothes in the latest fashion; oversize jewelry and more make up than she needed to wear, but Jessica had a face worthy of pageant competitions. Her four henchwomen were there, like clockwork, following her, not looking anything like her at all, but happy to be there for the ride, I presumed.

This was the same year that the President got sick at a dinner in Japan and that same year that the Los Angeles riots happened over the acquittal of the four cops who beat Rodney King.

I was taller than Jessica, but weak, and scared. My oversized clothing was supposed to make me pass incognito, but that girl never led up. She kept coming after me. From the first time she saw me in class.

I bent down to pick up my books and papers, but Jessica's foot was preventing me from doing so. That's when I realized that my problems were about to escalate as Jessica's friends surrounded me.

"So, *Pendeja*? Are you that messy at home? Start cleaning!"

I looked her in her eyes as Jessica looked in mine. Fear was looking at hate. Hate was looking down on fear as an evil master looking at their slave.

It's funny how you always notice someone's facial expression change as they're about to strike somebody down. As if the power required to give a defining blow came from your facial muscles.

And just as enough power had been generated in Jessica's face; it was all drained by surprise as she was flipped around.

"What the fuck is your problem Jessica?"

I got up, happy to see Maria. Jessica's henchwomen regrouped and moved away from me and followed their leader as she walked away, saying "Just helping the clumsy Mulatto."

"Pendeja," was the word I thought I heard Maria mutter under her breath as they walked away.

Turning to me, she said, "Pick up your books or you're going to be late for class."

I started to pick up my books and said, "Thank you,"

"You know she's only messing with you because she knows you're hotter than her."

"I try not to look pretty. I'm always wearing baggies," I replied still looking down.

"Renee, fuck that bitch! You've got it so flaunt it! Let that ugly duckling deal with her own issues."

"But is that why she hates me so much?"

"Maybe. People talked about her like she was some Goddess, but when you got in, a lot of folks started talking about how cute you were. Mixed breed kids always are a hot commodity."

Maria was trying to make me smile. I was not in the mood. I was still scared of Jessica.

"What can I do, Maria?"

"Just keep to yourself and don't let that *puta* push you around."

I went back to picking up my stuff on the ground and straightening it out saying, "I'll try."

Then things went the way they always went between me and Maria. Silence was the glue that held us together.

I don't know how long Maria was there looking at me picking up my mess. I think she stayed long enough to make sure that they were not going to come back and get me. But it took sometime before I heard the sound of her heels walking away from me.

I didn't want to look up. I felt ashamed. But when I did, the hallway was empty. The bell had rung and I was late for class.

I was out of class, notes taken and ready to for the next period.

And then, as I turned the corner to get to the stairs, I was knocked down on my ass. The impact created quite a shock, but the anticipation of more pain almost brought tears to my eyes as I thought that I would have to face Jessica and her crew, but to my surprise, I was helped back up to my feet. A young man said, "I'm so sorry. I should be looking where I'm going."

A red haired freckled face white guy was in front of me; probably about my age or a year older, wearing baggy clothes. He was strong and I could tell from the impact, but he didn't look it. Realizing my books were on the ground, once again, I went back to pick them up. He helped me and picked up a few. He said, "Hey, I've been noticing you. You're kind of quiet."

I looked into his green brown eyes and said, "I'm trying to keep a low profile."

He smiled and asked, "Are you famous?"

I noticed that he had feminine mannerisms. Could he be gay?

"I'm not famous. I just like it better that way."

"Low profile makes it easier to get by right?"

"I would like to think so."

I got up with my stuff in one arm. He extended his hand and said, "My name is Cooper."

I shook his hand saying, "I'm Renee."

"Nice to meet you. I find you SO pretty."

He was gay. I could tell. I smiled and started making my way to class. He asked, "Can I walk you to class?"

"Sure."

The 5 minutes it took to get to class, I had learned that he was a year older than me. He said that he had always noticed me, but never knew how to approach me. He was happy that we met. I was happy to make a friend. He seemed like a good guy.

In the meantime, I got detention for being late in class earlier.

I did my time by working on homework and assignments. It was only October and I really didn't want to get that type of reputation as a girl who spent time in detention. The people that were in detention were social misfits and socially awkward people; people who didn't have friends. Come to think of it, I could've been their queen.

Once detention was done, the school was quiet and empty. I had completed most of my work and I didn't want to bring my books back home, so I walked to my locker. That was a mistake. My unwelcoming party was there waiting for me. Fear was facing hatred again. After being pushed against lockers repeatedly, the last thing I remembered was that face Jessica made before punching me.

I came to in the hospital. My right arm was broken from trying to protect my face and I had a couple of broken ribs too. My face was a little bruised, but surprisingly enough, no major disfiguration.

I stayed in the hospital for two days. My mother could not afford to keep me there, or maybe she just didn't want to. It was one or the other.

I was asked who was responsible. I said that I didn't know. I was taught never to snitch. I never did.

I stayed home for a week, recovering, during that time, Maria would bring me my school work, little miss Straight A's. When I returned to school, for a week long, Maria would walk me back home, until the routine became monotone.

In the meantime, I was getting not so anonymous calls at home. Girls would call in and as soon as my mother picked up the phone, they'd ask to speak to me in the nicest possible voice, but once mama would give me the phone, the insults would start. Whore, Bitch, Puta, Pendeja, I even got Rusty Cunt Bucket. After I had my fill of derogatory comments, every time I'd pick the phone up, I'd hang up right away.

The week that Maria stopped walking me home, nothing happened for a week again. I made sure I made it to class on time and ran back home after school. I made sure that I always had my things ready before my last class so that I could leave right away.

But then, after a little while, the monotony hit me as well and I got careless. I went to my locker after my last class. My cast was present for another week, bandages were still the latest fashion for my sides, but my face was back to its original features with minor blemishes. You would think that with all these reminders on me, I'd be more alert.

Students were still walking around in the halls. Most of them were going to their extracurricular activities. I made my way out of school, enjoying the sweet Chicago wind, but not for long. The fastest way to my house was the doors on the west side of the school. Logic and instinct were not in sync that day. As I made it out, there they were, talking to each other. I was weak the first time they beat me up. I was a handicap at that point and time.

Jessica smiled and said, "Girls, look at this. Christmas came a month early this year."

They regrouped like the she wolves they were. My breathing increased along with my fears and with every step they made towards me. I closed my eyes this time before looking at Jessica building the strength from her face to pummel me. But then . . . Nothing happened. I waited and wondered if I got such a blow to the head that I couldn't feel anything else. I dared opening my eyes and they stayed there away from me looking towards the door, where a white kid was standing. He was just standing there, next to me, his face not wearing fear like mine was, or anger like Jessica's, but defiance with a smirk added on. I recognized him. It was the same gay white dude I met the day I got jumped. I didn't like my odds.

Jessica and her posse looked impatient. They were hungry and had to feed on my fear while it was at its highest. They needed him to go away.

Jessica made a face that asked *well?!?* And Cooper gave her a face that asked *what?!?* Once their faces stopped conversing, Jessica allowed her mouth to take over the conversation and said, "Move the fuck on, faggot!"

"I don't want to, bitch!"

Jessica tapped her foot on the concrete, hoping that he would eventually have to get somewhere. He didn't budge and she didn't like it at all. He was socially inferior to her, especially in a school where gays and Caucasians were a minority, but he didn't care about the hierarchy. He was Robin Hood and he had come to save me.

Jessica and her wolf pack walked away without saying a word to me or Cooper. Once they were at a safe distance, Cooper helped me up, his face now wearing compassion. He said, "Are you ok?"

"Thank you," I said with tears in my eyes.

He told me how he never really liked Jessica or her friends. He also said that Jessica would not try to attack him because he knew martial arts. I really didn't believe it until he asked, "Do you want me to train you? I mean, once you're healed and all."

As he talked, he still sounded like a woman. I could not believe that he could hurt anyone.

"What would you train me on?"

"Muay Thai and Jujitsu."

Apparently, he had been training for the past two years in both styles and claimed to be very good at it. From there, I agreed to train and learn how to defend myself with only one goal in mind . . . See Jessica's face.

CHAPTER 5

Pasteles

The smell of cooked up corn and spices was coming out of the Rodriguez kitchen on Christmas morning. Mama, Maria and I were getting things ready for Christmas dinner. Simon was on his way to spend Christmas with us and I wanted to make sure that the house was perfect since it was the first time he was formally invited to the house by my mother. If everything went accordingly, she'd agree to ring in 1999 at MY ADDICTION with all of us.

Simon and I started dating no longer than 4 days after meeting at the club. From the first date we had, I was being spoiled by Simon. He either bought me the most expensive things he could find or he'd bring me to the most extravagant events in town.

He knew of my affiliation with sports and took me out to see the Chicago Fire take on the Columbus crew for the soccer championship at Soldier Field. I never really was a big soccer fan, but the excitement in the air was just incredible. We went to sporting events, charity events and private parties.

I was not the only one reaping on the goods of that new life. Maria always had free access to the club and her seat was always in the VIP along with free drinks. Whenever she was intoxicated, she had a free limo ride back to her place or mama's house. She would also tag along to the events that were of interests to her.

As for Simon, he never complained. He never mentioned that we were taking advantage of him in anyway shape or form. I was not looking to take advantage of him though, but he was very adamant on the places where he wanted to go out. Was I falling in love with Simon? No! I was falling in like. Appreciating another human being again was definitely different for me. I missed that.

As our relationship progressed, I could sense that he was getting restless with me. Our first kiss had not happened before our 2nd month together and he stole that one. I became accustomed to kissing him at the end of every date after that robbery.

As a family tradition, all 3 of us women were cooking *Pasteles*, on christmas. The smell of grated vegetables, diced and ground meat spread throughout the house. Conversations were kept to a very low. *Pass this, pass that, move here, move there* . . . No laughter like in your family movies and no arguments like in your tragedies, although I was expecting the latter to happen as soon as Simon got in.

But pasteles was not the only dish being prepared. The chicken was already done and so was the rice which was cooked with vegetables and meat in it. The feast looked and smelled great once it was done.

As we had finished setting up the table, the door bell was heard. I looked at my mother who in turn looked at me as well. She nodded and I went to the door.

As I reached the door, I fixed up my clothes, a pair of slightly fitted jeans and a pink blouse I wore only on special occasions, making sure I was looking decent. I opened the door, only to find Simon standing outside with two other men. All of them had wrapped gifts and Christmas bags in hands, too many to count. Simon asked, "Where do we put these?"

My eyes had widened at the sight of Simon, surprised at his gesture. I turned around and saw my mother and sister sporting the same look I had on my face. I then looked at Simon again and said, "The Christmas tree is in the living room."

We had removed the couch from the living room and brought it upstairs and instead, we brought in the dining table from the kitchen along with four chairs for the meal. In a corner which was not crowded at the opposite side of the room, I directed Simon and his people to drop their offerings there, right under the Christmas tree.

After 2 more trips between the living room and the van outside, all the gifts had been delivered under the Christmas tree. Simon gave a $100 bill to each of his associate and said, "Thanks for your help, fellas. You have a Merry Christmas."

The gentlemen took their new found riches and left. An awkward moment of silence took control of the room. Esperanza, my mother, was giving a suspicious look to Simon, while Maria and I were looking at him with smiles. Simon asked, "So where do we go from here?"

Maria said, "Let's open the gifts!"

Esperanza said, sharply and still looking at Simon, "*¡No! ¡Comemos primero!*[5]"

Simon asked me, "What did that mean?"

"We gonna eat."

At this point, I was afraid that my mother was going to attempt to get rid of Simon. I hoped in my heart that nothing wrong would happen during dinner.

We all took our place at the table. I sat next to Simon on his right. Mama was across the table from him, while Maria was facing me.

Mama started, "*Permítanos orar.*[6]"

We all bowed our heads and closed our except for Simon. Ok, I didn't exactly close both my eyes. I kept looking on to make sure he understood what was going on. Once he imitated us, I closed both my eyes and waited.

The whole time, mama prayed in Spanish, thanking God for her health, for her family, asking for blessings for the meal, asking that Maria gets a good husband, that I get my head on straight and move right in life, asking for her husband's soul to be kept as well, asking the Holy Father to bless the rest of the evening, asking Him to bless her family back home, asking for world peace, and then I stopped listening and just waited.

Finally, she said, "Amen!"

Simon looked up smiling, proud that he had understood that. Mama said to Simon, in a strong Spanish accent, "Go ahead and eat. My daughters and I cooked this meal all day."

Simon went ahead and took some rice, some *pasteles* and some chicken in his plate. As he was still taking in food, he looked at the 3 of us as we were, once again, looking at him. He obviously didn't get it. He asked, "Did I do something wrong?"

Smiling, I said, "We don't eat until the guests finished serving themselves."

---

5 No! We eat first!

6 Let's pray.

"Oh!" said Simon. He then looked at his plate and looked up again, and said, smiling, "I'm done!"

"Finally!" said Maria.

She then proceeded to serve herself, and mama and I followed her.

As everyone had their plates filled with the wonderful food on the table, mama sat there, watching Simon, as he ate. Smiling, she said, "It's nice that you came and spent Christmas with us. I know you came to see Dolores, but you know Maria is single."

Simon looked at me and then Maria and then back at me. I refused to get into it. She first was complaining about him not being right for me and now, she probably thought he was too good for me. Maria, after swallowing the last bite she had, said, "Mama, I am not interested in Simon."

She then winked at me and said, "He can't handle me."

I smiled and went back to eating until I heard my mother again, "The two of you should at least try dating before jumping to conclusion."

I dropped my fork on my plate. I had heard enough. She should at least try to do that while I was not in the room, not in my face as if I was not existent. I said, "I'm sorry mama, but he likes me and not Maria. Maria has enough to keep her busy. No offense Maria!"

"Don't worry *querida*. None taken," said Maria.

Mama looked at both Maria and I and said, putting down her fork, "I don't think you can handle a relationship and school at the same time Dolores."

My anger started to rise, and it could be heard as my breathing started to intensify. Maria seeing this, started, "*Mamá, eso es bastante ahora. Disfrutemos del alimento.*[7]"

Mama said going back to her plate, "*Acabo de la decir la verdad.*[8]"

Maria looked at me as I took a deep breath and just like my mother, went back to eating. Simon just kept looking on in amazement. I looked at him and as soon as his eyes locked in with mine, I said, "Eat."

Simon obeyed. I like to think that he thought it would be best to do so as he didn't want to start any more arguments with me.

The rest of the dinner was like that. The only sound made was the forks and knives knocking against our plates as we consumed the food.

---

7 Mama, that's enough. Let's enjoy the food now.

8 I am just telling her the truth.

The same atmosphere that we had in the kitchen as we made this meal possible had followed us to what was now the dining room. Simon, easily, was able to follow along on our little choreography of silence. Asking for water or juice, asking for salt, passing a plate to who asked for it, taking a plate for whoever heard him request it. Gotta love Christmas!

Finally, as Simon finished, he sat back in his seat and let out a big sigh, breaking the silence that we were all so used to. He then said, adding more noise to our cold war, "Wow! You women are a triple threat! That was good!"

Simon looked over at everyone's plate to make sure that they had all finished their food and after being able to confirm it all, he asked, "Can we move to the gift section now?"

Maria and I turned to mama. She said, "*Permítanos clara la mesa primero*[9]."

After hearing that, the two of us started clearing the table. Mama helped as well. Simon got up and picked up his plate, which was then taken from him by me. As his hand touched the plate of pasteles, Maria took that away from him. Finally, he tried to take the bowl of rice, but Esperanza slapped his hand and said, "You can help Dolores move the table when it's cleared."

Simon then went back to his seat and watched as the table went from having a few plates and glasses to a white table cloth with a gold trim, which after being taken away showed a perfectly varnished cherry wooden table. Simon got up as I walked in saying, "Grab the other end of the table."

Simon went ahead and held his end of the table. We brought the table to the side of the room which was opposite to the gifts. Then, we moved the 4 chairs which were used during dinner and placed them one next to another, facing the Christmas tree.

Then, we sat on two of the empty chairs, next to one another, waiting for Maria and mama to finish in the kitchen. Simon looked at the gifts and said, "I hope they like my gifts."

I looked his way and asked, "Do I get a gift?"

Simon flashed his signature smile and held my hand. He then said, "You'll see."

I smiled and asked, playfully, "Oh really?"

---

9 Let's clear the table first.

I kissed his cheek, but then pulled away quickly as I heard my mother and sister coming back in the room with a few packages.

They dropped them along with Simon's gift in the corner of the room and sat on the chairs. Simon looked at them and asked, "So how do you guys usually do this?"

Maria said, going into her pocket, "We usually start giving the gift to the oldest and we keep going down."

She pulled out a small box wrapped up in red and white foiling. She then went into her other pocket and took out a bow, which she stuck on the on box. She then gave the box to mama and said, "*Esto es para usted, mama.*[10]"

Smiling, Esperanza picked up the gift and said, "*Gracias, mi hija!*"

She then opened the box and pulled out a pair of silver earrings, shaped in a heart with a diamond in the centre. Of course the diamonds weren't real, for the earrings were knock-offs. The silver painting on the hearts was not applied properly as some parts showed the copper that it was supposed to cover.

The smile on her face grew as she saw them and then went and hugged Maria. I looked on, envying that I would get that type of response one day, instead of critics.

Simon got up saying, "Well, it's time for our gift."

He went to pick up a small box wrapped in red and white, saying, "This was from me and Renee."

He gave the box to mama. She looked at it and looked at me. I bit my lower lip looking at her with my hands clasped together, hoping that she would see the effort I put in getting that gift. I thought hard of something that would make her happy and I stopped at nothing to get this for her.

Mama unwrapped her gift and was faced with a red velvet box. Again, she looked at me and said, "That seems to be very expensive."

She then looked at Simon and smiled. Mama then opened the box and I held my breath waiting for a reaction from my mother.

Mama held one hand to her mouth. That gave me hope of something positive. Maria looked on as well and took out a pearl necklace from inside, saying, "Renee, how much dough you spent on that?"

---

[10] This is for you, mama.

Mama snapped at her and said, "*¡Maria! ¡No sea ridículo! ¡Obviamente, el hombre negro pagó por ello!*[11]"

What? My look changed from anticipating the one reaction I wanted from my mother to sheer disappointment. I said, "Actually, mother, I paid for it. Simon only paid for the gift wrap."

She said to me, "We'll talk about it later, Dolores."

Disappointment fled. It had no place in me because my anger moved in. The scowl on my face showed that. I crossed my arms and said, "Whatever!"

Simon looked at us all in the room, feeling the tension. Maria, who was used to such situations in the house, started, "Let's get back to gift giving. Who's the oldest after mama?"

Simon looked around and raised his hand like a shy little boy on his first day of school. And the distribution of gifts continued, as if what my mother said had not been uttered. I was hurt, but I was not going to let her ruin this special Christmas.

Simon got a card from Maria and mama, while I bought him a pair of golden cuff links. Maria received a $100 from mama while I gave her a new dress. Simon gave her a CD player with brand new CDs of her favourite artists.

And then came my turn. I received $50 from my mother and sex toys from Maria which my mother ordered to go in the trash. I couldn't help but laugh because Maria did that just to cause a stir.

When came time for Simon to give his gifts, a few of the boxes had not been opened.

Simon said to me, "I wanted to keep the best for last, so I won't give you my gift just yet. Before all that, I got gifts for the entire family."

I looked at Maria thinking that she might be involved in this gift giving surprise. Maria returned the same surprised look showing that she was totally clueless over this issue. I didn't bother looking at mama because I knew that she would never be part of a surprise for me.

So I looked on as Simon displayed gifts which were intended for the entire family; a sound system, TV, VCR, DVD Player, microwave and a house computer.

Finally, two bags were remaining. Simon said, "Like I said before, I saved the best for last."

---

[11] Maria! Don't be ridiculous! Obviously, the black man paid for it!

I looked at him, arms still crossed. He picked up both bags and sat on his chair. Looking at me, he said, "I remember that first night we talked and you told me that you wanted to be Claire Huxtable in the courtroom."

He then pulled out from one bag a solid grey double breasted cashmere suit with three small buttons to fasten the suit. The same amounts of buttons were found on the sleeve cuffs. Slanted flap pockets were placed on both sides of the jacket. The skirt was very straight and simple with a tiny slit at the back. From the other bag, he pulled out a black leather briefcase.

I held one hand to my mouth shocked from seeing that same outfit I had seen in one of the episode. It was a dream come true. All I needed was Dr. Huxtable. Without thinking, I went ahead and hugged him overwhelmed with joy.

Everyone shared in that moment, except for mama. She snapped, "*¡Dolores, eso no es manera para una chica de actuar delante de su madre!*[12]"

I pulled away from Simon whispering in his ear, "Thank you."

I then sat back down under the watchful eye of my mother. She barked, "*Usted quiere ser un vagabundo pequeño, hágalo fuera de la casa de mi marido. Yo no lo aceptaré.*[13]"

The phone then rang. Saved by the bell, I thought, because I knew that mama was not going to be done ranting on my behavior. Before that first ring even ended, I jumped saying, "I'll get it!"

As I walked away towards that ring, I smiled inside a little bit because I was able to walk away before my mother killed this special moment created by Simon.

I reached the phone at the third ring. I picked up and said, "Hello?"

A female voice responded, "Hi . . ."

I waited. The voice sounded familiar, but I could really not tell from just a *hi.* I asked, "Can I help you?"

The woman asked, "Are you The Shark's girl?"

The voice was really familiar now. I took a moment prior to answering that, trying to think and see if where I possibly could've heard that voice before. The fact that she mentioned Simon by his nickname told me that

---

[12] Dolores, that's no way for a girl to act in front of her mother!

[13] You want to be a little tramp, do it outside of my husband's house. I will not accept it.

she must've been someone from the club. One of the girl's who saw me once maybe? Not being able to come up with anyone I could associate to the voice, I asked, "Who wants to know?"

The woman on the phone said sharply, "Your replacement, bitch!"

I was angry. This did not seem like a joke and I had not allowed anyone to call me names like that one since my days back in school. I shouted, "Motherfucker, you come to my face and say that shit! You got the number, I'm sure you can find the address, bitch!"

"*¡No te enojes porque soy mejor que tú!*[14]"

At that time, I had heard about enough. I was not one to use words when it was obviously a fight she was looking for. I hung up on the woman and stayed by the phone with my head down, breathing loudly as I remembered my youth in high school when those girls kept calling my house to terrorize me. I remembered crying by myself having that feeling that I was hated by everyone.

I could not even begin to understand how all of that started, until I remembered the girl asking if I was The Shark's girlfriend. It was time to go shark hunting. I called out, "Simon!"

Simon hurried over. As he reached next to me, he said, "I am so happy you called me out here. Your mother is sweating me in there."

I still had my head down and my back turned to him. I knew that if I looked at him, we were going to fight. Not a verbal fight. We were going to physically fight because he would have to fight me if he wanted to survive what I wanted to do right now. Simon, asked with confusion in his voice, "Baby, are you ok?"

"Some bitch called here saying that she was my replacement!" I snapped, still looking down.

"They replaced you at work?"

The motherfucker was trying to be funny. I turned around facing him with tears in my eyes, and yelled out, "*Pendejo!* Stop acting stupid!"

Simon, confused, said, "I am not acting. What are you talking about?"

I said, wiping my tears, "This ho called me saying that she was going to replace me as your girlfriend."

"What?" said Simon, "You got her name?"

---

[14] Don't be angry because I am better than you!

"Why should it matter what her name is? That bitch calls me out my name talking about she better than me and shit!"

Simon moved towards me, arms opened, attempting to take me in his arms saying, "You need to calm down baby!"

I didn't want to be held. I didn't want to be calmed down. I wanted to fight. I pushed him away, screaming, "Don't tell me to calm down!"

Simon took a deep breath. He then asked, "Can I talk to you without having you at my throat?"

I said sharply, crossing my arms, "Go ahead!"

Simon took a deep breath and said, "First of all, I have no idea who it is that could call you. You know a bunch of people wanna be in your spot right now and they'll do anything to end what we have."

At that point, I was scowling. I asked, "How did she get my phone number?"

Simon answered, "I have no idea! But I wish I knew who she was. I'd get you to whoop her ass!"

With arms crossed, my look hadn't changed. I was still angry and Simon's attempt of a joke had failed. Maria arrived and asked, "Mama sent me over here cause we can't hear you guys yelling anymore. What's going on?"

I hadn't flinched and Simon hadn't moved either. However, my stillness was caused by anger, while Simon's was caused by fear.

I said, "Leave, right now!"

Simon asked, "Can't we talk about this?"

I shouted, "LEAVE!"

Simon bit his lower lip and started making his way towards the door. Before turning the knob, he turned around and said, "Give your mother my regards. I'll be at the club if you end up looking for me."

He then left.

I stayed in place with my eyes low, trying to make sense of everything. Maria came closer, squatted, attempting to look into my eyes, saying, "You okay, *querida*?"

I said, "Star 69 the last number and 411 the address for it."

Maria and I knew each other well enough to know why I was asking her to do that. She smiled as she went to the phone singing, "We are going to beat a bitch's ass!"

I, meanwhile, went upstairs and changed into black sweat pants, a black sweater and runners. I put my hair in a pony tail and then did about 30 push ups. I felt that I had every right to go after that girl. She was just as evil as the bitches I went to school with. I was not going to let that continue. I was going to teach someone a lesson.

After shadow boxing with my reflection in the full length mirror in my room, I put on a large black Chicago Bulls coat and went back downstairs. There Maria was still by the phone, writing on a paper.

I asked, "So? Where did the call come from?"

Maria had a concerned look on her face. She said, "My Addiction night club."

The smell of pasteles was still in the air as I said in my anger, "Let's go!"

CHAPTER 6

Confirmed

The car ride was not a quiet one as Maria kept switching from English to Spanish mentioning how she was ready to cause serious injuries to Simon and that mystery woman on the phone.

Me, on the other hand, was just quiet, wondering how I could've been so stupid to let him into my life, my world; my secured world. I was not in love with the guy, but I still had this sense of entitlement and that's when my thoughts shifted to the other woman. How bold was she to call MY home and advise ME of the status of MY relationship? I still tried to figure out who she was. I went through all the Spanish women that worked for the club and I couldn't figure out who that was.

I was so deep in my thoughts that I had not realized that we made our way through traffic and were already at the club. The 25 minutes ride to get to the club didn't even seem that long.

The club's parking lot was as deserted as any day I came while the club had not opened its doors, but this time was more special. I came to do battle in there. We stepped out the car and the wind was strong and against me, as if to tell me to turn back. I was too angry to agree with my dearest wind. I was too angry to be reasonable.

Maria and I went through the back door as we would usually do, but again, things felt different for me. I remembered watching Scarface when Tony Montana was going in to ambush his boss who tried to take him out. We were going in to ambush a bitch who thought she could take my spot when I was willing to give it to her . . . violently.

The two of us were gangsters wearing our Chicago Bulls black bomber jacket with the red bull in the back without the guns. In the angry state I was in, I knew that I was a lethal weapon. Probably couldn't take on the guards, but definitely could beat any girl any day.

At the back of the building was an elevator that led straight to the 6th level of the club. That was the administrative level. There was no dancing or drinks being served up there. Only music played in that level was your typical classical music and only drinks served were coffee, tea, water or hot chocolate.

As we stood in the slow ass elevator, Maria looked at me real quiet at first. Her look then turned into a stare. I tried to ignore it, but then as she kept going, I got annoyed and asked, "What?"

"You must really care about this dude."

"How you figure?"

Maria leaned on the wall opposite me and said, "Well, I came along cause I care for you and don't like you being hurt and also cause I enjoy a good beat down from time to time."

"I think the beat down portion was your only reason."

She laughed and asked, "What about you?"

The elevator signaled that we arrived on our floor and before the door opened, I said, "I'm here to beat down a girl who thinks she can disrespect me while I'm at home, nothing more, nothing less. If Simon gets involved, he'll get his too."

Maria started laughing and the doors opened to a lobby with red couches on the right and left. The floor was carpeted with a blue and dark grey carpet. In front of us were two sandblasted glass doors which led to many offices and departments. At those doors, there were Eugene and Benjamin, Simon's two guards, wearing black suits and sunglasses.

Eugene was the tall and buffed guard who refused entry to Maria the first night we came to *My Addiction*. Benjamin was a guard that looked just like the boxer Eric 'Butterbean' Esch.

We got a chance to get acquainted with Eugene on a more friendly level over the past few weeks. Maria was still attempting to get him to sleep with her.

Maria and I walked up to the glass doors. As we reached, I said, "Hey Eugene! What's up Ben?"

Eugene replied, "Hi."

While Ben just answered with a head nod. I asked Eugene, "Is he in?"

Eugene answered, "I haven't seen him yet. I talked to him on the phone a few minutes ago and he sounded pissed off."

I looked at Maria who with a look of her own acknowledged that it was in relation to what happened earlier at their house.

To make sure, I asked, "Did he come to his office at all today?"

He shook his head no.

"Thanks," I then lied, "I have to get something of mine in there. I'll get it and get back out real quick."

Eugene said, "Okay. You will meet the secretary that I hired earlier today. She won't bother you."

I looked at Maria again. Maria smiled at me with one sinister smile knowing that we now had a suspect . . .

The two goons opened the glass doors. I led the way while Maria stayed behind. She then said, to Eugene "Are you sure that I can't make you sway my way?"

"Sweetheart, I only love men who can give it to me strong," he said winking at her.

Maria stood there, mouth opened, in awe. She was about to say something, but I pulled her inside the office area saying, "Get in here!"

I didn't have to lie to the club staff as I had carte blanche on everything I wanted. I never took advantage of those privileges unless Maria was around.

Behind the glass doors was a long narrow corridor with 3 doors on the left side and 3 doors on the right. About 20 feet ahead was the main door made of sandblasted glass as well which was Simon's office.

As the doors closed behind us, I was a woman on a mission, opening every office door that was in my path, looking for someone specific. Realizing later, that whoever I was looking for was in the room facing me, I went ahead and entered Simon's office.

The giant mahogany desk was facing me. Behind the desk was a brown leather chair with a giant view of the city behind it. A few shelves on each side of the room were there. The office in itself could fit two rooms in Mama's house. On the desk, there was a computer monitor, with papers, a letter opener, some pens, a rolodex, envelopes, two desk trays and a bookend.

Right next to the desk though, with papers in her hand, was a young woman standing there, dressed in a black skirt and white shirt. As we walked in, the young lady said, “Hi! Can I help you?”

I recognized the voice and looked the girl over. She couldn’t have been over 110 lbs. The girl was very attractive and did look Hispanic. A little shorter than Maria, but she didn’t look like she could fight. I knew she couldn’t fight. She just had a loud mouth.

Maria said, sounding as shocked as I looked, “Jessica?”

But then the memories erased that shocked look I had. The same girl I ended up fighting in school, she stood there looking in my eyes and me looking in hers and I recognized the look she had, the same way she recognized my look. It was a look we shared many years ago, in high school, after I was confident enough to go beat her ass. It was 6 months after Cooper rescued me. I was no longer scared and I wanted to get her back. I followed her, risking detention and I found out her schedule. I recognized a pattern. She had to go to the bathroom every class she had. Thirty minutes into the class she would go to meet her crew in the bathroom to talk for 15 minutes and then return.

After a week of staking out her habits, I finally made my move. It was during second period. She walked towards the bathroom but never made it there. She turned that corner and I grabbed a handful of her precious lock of hair. I swung her ass against the lockers and began throwing punches and elbows. She covered her face the whole time. Her ribs felt it though. But I had the opportunity to look her in the eyes. She looked me in mine. Unlike me, she was not afraid. Jessica’s hatred for me matched my hatred for her. Seeing that defiance of my power over hers angered me more. I gave one final punch in her ribs and I left. She was later found by a teacher who brought her to the infirmary. She didn’t spend the night at the hospital. I hadn’t beaten Jessica that badly, but I made sure she’d always remember it. I was never called to the office. She never spoke. But through our four years of high school together, we had many conflicts. Our eyes always seemed to meet and a barrage of insults always rose between us. She never tried to fight me again though, nor did her little crew attempt to be brave and try me. I kept training and I never saw the need to go after her again, but the insults and the hatred remained until we parted ways on that last day of school.

When I found her in Simon's office, things had not changed. They say actions speak louder than words, but our looks were louder than any actions or words.

I said, closing the door behind me, "As a matter of fact, you can help me."

I then walked towards the girl, grabbed Jessica by her shirt, lifted her up, moved her towards the closed door and held her against it saying, "*¿Así que usted es supuesto ser mi remplazó?*[15]"

She put her hands on my wrist attempting to overpower me, but to no avail. I was obviously still too strong for her. She said, "You don't deserve to be with The Shark. I am a better woman than you'll ever be."

Maria said, "*Renee, la parada que pierde el tiempo y permite que nosotros golpear su culo ya.*[16]"

I said, "I have a few questions first."

I then looked at the young girl and asked, "How long?"

Jessica, still struggling to get free, said, now not sounding scared anymore, "How long what, *puta*?"

As a desperation move, the young lady slapped me in the face. I growled as I flung her towards the desk behind me, making the young girl knock over the monitor, the leather chair and desk trays. I took off my jacket and walked towards the young girl again. After moving the chair out of my way, I lifted her up and held her against the desk this time. I said in a more stern tone, "How long has this been going on?"

Jessica smiled, which angered me more. The girl said, "It has not started yet, but don't worry, it won't take long for him to see that he's wasting his time with you. That's when he'll come running to me."

I looked at her, and said, "You're still the same crazy bitch."

"And you're still a bitch."

Maria, who was in a safe corner of the office, holding on to my jacket, asked, "So let me get this straight, you didn't even speak to Simon and yet, you trying to break him up with his girlfriend so you could have him to yourself?"

She snarled at Maria, "That's none of your business!" She then said to me, "You better let go of me now or I'm going to hurt you."

---

[15] So you're supposed to be my replacement?

[16] Renee, stop wasting time and let's beat her ass already.

I looked at Maria with a look that said *am I hearing this correctly?* Maria returned the same look and a chuckle.

In the meantime, neither I nor Maria paid attention to Jessica who was franticly moving her hand across the desk. She swung at my face, but I was clever enough not to get hit twice and got my arm in the way. However, my forearm got cut. She had grabbed a letter opener and used it as a weapon. As though I was not affected by the wound I received (I was), I twisted Jessica's arm behind her back and squeezed. The girl screamed from the pain and dropped the letter opener. With my other hand, I grabbed the girl by her thighs and flipped her over the desk again. The pretty vixen landed on her back moaning. I looked at my arm and saw blood coming out. It was a pretty bad cut.

In the meantime, Maria was still in her corner, screaming out insults in Spanish. The girl tried to get up by holding on to the door handle. As she stood up on her feet, I walked around the desk, angrier now that I was wounded, and as I was close enough to the girl, I performed a perfect round house kick which made contact with Jessica's chest. Jessica went through the glass door and found herself in the corridor.

The sound of the breaking glass must have alerted the guards that were at the door because they all came running to the horrific scene along with Simon. Standing about 3 feet away from us, Simon asked, "What the fuck is going on here?"

I picked Jessica up again and held her up against the wall, since she was still groggy from the impact she suffered a little earlier. I then said to Simon, as she stayed in my grasp almost lifeless, "This is my replacement. I'm just giving her the proper lesson on how to replace me."

I then kneed the girl in her stomach, which caused her to gasp loudly.

Simon asked, "Eugene, who is this girl?"

He answered, "That's Jessica Ramirez. The agency sent her to work as your secretary. I would've told you earlier, but you didn't seem in the mood."

I looked at Eugene, shocked. So Simon was unaware of her being here. Some anger started to sip out of me and guilt began to settle in.

Simon said to me, "Baby, let her go, or it might do you more wrong for your career."

He then turned to the guard again. I had not listened. I couldn't hear anything. I didn't have friends, nor did I have people that I hated, but

Jessica, I did hate. I hated her more than anything for the torture I suffered back in school, for that trip to the hospital.

I snapped back to reality once I heard, "Renee, sweetheart, you can let go of the girl."

Everyone was looking at me. Jessica's motionless body was still against the wall supported by my hands. I took deep breaths as I was really into the moment. The anger from the phone call earlier had brought me to a high level, but once I saw who it was . . . Once I saw Jessica standing there, I got back to that high school day when I had beaten her up.

I released her from my grip and Jessica dropped on the ground, almost like dead weight, still groaning in pain.

I was embarrassed because Simon told me that he didn't know her. Jessica confirmed not knowing him and Eugene also said that she had just started. I was just being jealous and caused a lot of damage. I looked at the carnage I had created and caused in my jealous rage and I was just shocked at how crazy I got.

Simon asked, "So how did you figure out who she was and where the call was made from?"

Maria said, coming out of the broken glass door proudly, "I Star 69'd the bitch!"

Simon looked at his door and the girl on the floor, with one hand on his hip and the other one rubbing the back of his head. Under his breath, he whispered, "Aaah, shit!"

I took my coat from Maria and walked towards Simon. I hugged him and whispered in his ear, "I'm sorry."

Simon kissed me and said, "It's ok. It won't cost much to replace it all. I was looking to move shit around anyway."

He then looked at my arm and saw the wound. He turned towards the guards and said to Benjamin, "Have this injury looked at. Eugene, get the other girl some medical attention, and then come see me."

Our backs turned, we were ready to go when we just heard a muffled mooing sound. We turned and saw Jessica on the floor, holding on to her sides. Maria said walking passed us, "I just needed to get one kick in."

CHAPTER 7

Honest Mistake

"You didn't have to beat Jessica up that badly."

Cooper and I were at the gym getting ready for another training session. He had stayed quiet the entire time. As soon as I laid myself down on the blue mat and rose my right leg for him to help me stretch it, he started with that bullshit. I had left the school after I had beaten her up. She was not going to talk to anybody and I was not going to be caught.

"If a teacher had seen you, what do you think would've happened?"

I hadn't told him what I had done. I just did it. He knew it was me as soon as he heard Jessica was sent to the nurse's office though.

He continued, as I raised my left leg for him to stretch as well, "I didn't teach you Muay Thai for you to start terrorizing people."

"I decided to learn it because of Jessica, remember?"

He stayed quiet. It was his turn to be stretched and he went through the same routine I went through, while I applied the necessary pressure for him.

My goal when I decided to learn to defend myself was to first thank Jessica personally. I was not going to kill her, but I was going to make her feel what I felt. It pissed me off that she was not scared. It pissed me off that she gave me that look of defiance instead of fearing me. I should've sent her to the hospital, but I believed that I got my point across.

Once Cooper's legs were done stretching, he rose up fast with his hands up. He caught my face. At first, I thought that it was some sort of drill where I had to learn to get out of, but then his lips kissed mine.

It was the most awkward of moments. I mean, gay men don't kiss women. Why was he kissing me?

Once he released his hold and looked at me, I'm pretty sure my eyes were wide opened and my mouth was not closed. My only question to him was, "What was that?"

"I . . . I'm sorry. I . . ."

"Are you not gay?"

He looked shocked, surprised and I could tell that he felt a little insulted. "Why would you think I was gay?"

Now, I started stammering.

"I'm . . . You see . . ."

"Wait, you thought I was gay all this time?"

I nodded. He bit his lower lip. He then stood up and said, "I'm sorry then. I thought that maybe you felt what it is that I felt."

He got up and continued stretching on his own leaving me to think.

What did he feel about me? Why would he feel that about me? I mean, we were good friends, but romance between the two of us? Would it work out? Plus, he was the white guy at school and I was the lonely half breed? Would that help our case?

I didn't know what to think. I was flattered, but then I wondered . . . Why me?

CHAPTER 8

Anniversary

"How's College treating you?"

Mr. Samuels' question took me by surprise. I had not cared for school in quite a while. I missed a few classes and the hardest one; I just failed a test for it. I tried to lie. I mean, he was not my father, but I knew he'd be disappointed.

"It's . . . Fine . . . I guess"

"You guess?"

My mouth was opened and I wanted to say something, but I didn't know. I didn't want to lie to Mr. Samuels. I just stayed there, mouth opened. He was able to guess what was going on.

"You got to keep away from them distractions little girl. You have too much potential to throw it away like that."

"Yes sir."

"I hope you'll turn it around."

"Yes sir."

He continued his conversation and picked up his usual items. He stayed until the next customer walked in.

I was at work, working the afternoon shift on Valentine's Day. I had already called Simon and wished him a happy valentine's day. I wanted to go home and catch up on my reading. Mr. Samuels was right. I had been putting school on the back burner to make space for romance in my life and it was time for me get focused on what was important.

My coworker was scheduled to come in for 8 pm & it was already 7:58 pm. A minute passed, and the door opened. Linda's young and blonde Caucasian frame walked in the convenience store. She looked almost identical to Gwyneth Paltrow in *Shakespeare In Love*. The young lady said, "Sorry for coming in so late Renee! I was held back by one of my many wannabe boyfriends."

Linda was another one like Maria. Except that she didn't try to hustle men out of their money. She just loved the attention she had from them. Sex was the only form of validation she required from those men and she was getting plenty of it.

I looked at her, shook my head as I let out a sigh and then said, "No biggie Linda. I get to leave, so I'm cool! If you had come 10 minutes later, I would've busted your ass though."

Linda asked, "Why 10 minutes?"

"That's when my bus comes in, sweetie."

Linda with a confused look asked, "Why do you bother with the bus when your boyfriend owns the biggest club in Chicago? Why do you bother with this job?"

I walked towards the storage room saying, "Because my boyfriend is busy and I don't want to disturb him with the type of shit that I'm used to deal with. As for the job, I would be heartbroken not to have you around in my life."

I looked back just to see what kind of face Linda would make at my sarcastic comment and she didn't disappoint. She was making a kid like grimace and I just chuckled.

In the storage room, I picked up my school bag, looked around to make sure I didn't forget anything and then made my way out. Linda was right. As The Shark's girlfriend, I had the right to every single perks this city could offer. I just had no desire to take them. I didn't want to take advantage of him.

As I walked out, I heard giggling, obviously from Linda. Thinking that she was on the phone talking to one of her many boyfriends, I decided to shrug it off, and started to hurry for my bus, but then stopped dead in my tracks as I saw Simon standing there at the counter in front of Linda, whispering in her ear

Anger started to rise up, fueled by jealousy. I was not used to jealousy. I had not learned how to control myself with such feelings. I never had to before. I didn't feel so strong about Simon, but he was my man.

I walked up to them, held Simon's arm and flipped him around so that he could face me. Simon looked at me, shocked.

Stammering, he started, "B . . . Baby! I . . . You see . . . I was . . . , I thought . . . I thought you finished earlier!"

I looked at him, not even hearing the words he just uttered. I was mad, angry and hurt. Why though? I wanted to cry. I really did, but I was not going to allow my humiliation to be shown through tears! I was not going to allow myself to be brought down like this by this one man who had gotten access to my world. I started, "What the fuck is going on here Simon? You were planning on stepping out on me at my job?"

I pointed at Linda and shouted, "And with that bitch?"

Simon held my arm, leading me outside, and saying, "I believe that we should take this outside right now."

I followed, because I wanted to let him have it. I was ready to let out all of my bottled up anger inside. Simon was going to be on the receiving end of an explosion, which was triggered by his disloyal actions, but the magnitude of it was the result of all the hurt and pain I had suffered throughout my life.

But as we stepped outside, a red carpet was laid out from the entrance of the convenience store to a limousine parked in front of the establishment. My anger changed to confusion. I turned to Simon who had his signature smile on his face, which made me more confused. *What was happening*, I wondered. As I was about to ask him, Linda came out of the store saying, "Happy 4 month anniversary and happy Valentine's Day!"

My confusion now changed to shame. I got duped by my boyfriend and co-worker. I just looked down and went to Simon and hugged him, as tight as I could, because I knew I was at fault. I whispered in his ears, "Baby, I'm sorry!"

Simon whispered back, "Don't worry. I was hoping for that reaction."

I said, still whispering, "No, I have to make it up to you, baby! Really, I have to."

Simon pulled back a little bit, put both his hands on my face and said, "If you want to make it up to me, you'll go to dinner with me."

"Now?"

"Yes, now."

I thought about Mr. Samuels' disappointed look when he left the store earlier and the fact that I had to get some studying done, but then again,

Simon went through a lot to surprise me. And after all, it is one night that we'll get to spend together, on Valentine's Day, on OUR anniversary.

I'd be able to get some studying done later, I told myself. Valentine's Day & anniversaries on the SAME day come along only once. It was only one night. Mr. Samuels would understand if he found out.

I smiled at Simon and said, "I'll go to dinner with you."

I then apologized to Linda for the insults I threw and Simon then held my hand and walked me to the limousine while Linda made her way back inside the store. For a minute, I realized something that was weird about today. The wind was not blowing, at all. I wondered if it was mad at me. I was then pulled out of my thoughts and inside the limousine.

As soon as the limousine door closed behind us, over filled with joy, I couldn't help but jump on Simon kissing him. I felt like he deserved it. I could've tried and told myself that I didn't care for him as much, but he's always shown me this form of appreciation. It was hard not to like him. It had been long since I could admit that I was developing feelings for someone.

Simon, hardly able to make his words come out, started, "Baby . . . I'm . . . Hold on."

I looked at him and said, breathing loudly, "I can't help it. I'm just so turned on by you right now. What you did just got me in all kinds of ways. *Yo sólo quiero besarte*[17]."

He looked at me with a look of desire in his eyes and said, "I love it when you speak Spanish to me. What did that mean?"

"I wanna kiss you . . . *Deseo que este momento pueda durar para siempre*[18]*!*"

Simon kissed me. I liked to think that the sound of my voice added to the words gave him goose bumps.

After a few minutes of kissing, the car came to a full stop. I asked, "Are we at the dinner place already?"

"No, we're not," said Simon fixing himself up.

"Where are we then?"

Simon stepped out the limousine and said, "Come out and see."

He opened my door and I looked out. To my surprise, we were facing the L.Y.D. (Live Your Dreams) store located on North Michigan Avenue,

---

17 I want to kiss you

18 I wish this moment could last forever

better known as LYD. I stayed in the limousine looking because I would never dare try to buy something from that store even when they had sales as I never had the money to afford anything they had.

Simon took me by the hand and started walking with me inside. I looked at Simon and he said to me as we walked in, "I have a gift for you, baby."

As we made a few steps inside the store, 3 women in black & white suits lined themselves up in front of us. One had a clipboard in her hands, the other had scissors and measuring tools, while the third lady was holding a comb and a makeup kit.

I looked at Simon and I could see that this wasn't part of his surprise because he was just as surprised as I was. I wondered what we were in store for.

The lady with the clipboard made one step towards us and said to Simon, "Welcome to L.Y.D.! We are happy to have you here! Is she the lucky lady?"

I looked at Simon again. Simon answered, unsure, "Are you . . . are you sure you got the right people? Cause we're not getting married."

The words scared me. I liked Simon, but marriage was scary.

I said, "Yeah! We are NOT getting married! We are just going to dinner . . ."

I then looked at Simon again, but with a smile this time and said, "I hope!"

Simon smiled and so did the lady with the clipboard. She looked in her clipboard and said looking at it, "According to my schedule, that's exactly what we have; Dinner preparations!"

Simon said, "Well, in that case, yes! She is the lucky lady!"

The lady asked, "What is your name?"

"Renee Rodriguez," I answered.

The lady said pointing at her look-a-likes, "These ladies will be assisting in making you ready for your dinner preparations."

Pointing at the lady with the scissors and measuring tape, she said, "This is Suzy. She will be taking care of the dress, handpicked by the gentleman who will be escorting you tonight. She will make all the alterations necessary so that the dress fits you perfectly."

Pointing at the lady with the comb and make up kit, she said, "This is Mandy. She will be taking care of your make up and your hair."

"I am Cindy! I will be supervising the entire operation."

Cindy then clapped her hands together 3 times and a scrawny looking gentleman dressed in the same colors as the other women walked in with a dark dress. The color was actually matching Simon's suit. I looked at the dress, speechless. Cindy continued, "This is our Satin Halter Gown. A silk charmeuse halter gown with pleating details on the bust as you can see and also with a back zip. This dress is from our *Carmen Marc Valvo* collection."

I was very much impressed by the look of the dress. I was mostly impressed by Simon's tastes in clothes. He needed a stylist so he could be wearing more suits than the one he was wearing now, but he definitely had a feel for women clothing as well.

Cindy continued, "Now, if you feel like we should go a certain way, please let us know. We will do our best to accommodate your needs during this whole experience. Any questions or concern can be directed to me."

Cindy then walked towards Simon and took him by the hand. She led him to a chair in some sort of lounging area, which was right by the cashier. There, there was a 35" plasma TV showing the Chicago Bulls playing and losing against the San Antonio's Spurs 17-11 after 1 quarter of playing time which was a big change from the year before when Michael Jordan, Scottie Pippen and Dennis Rodman used to rule the court with undeniable perfection.

As Simon sat down, Cindy said to him, "You can wait here and do not worry. You'll soon be mesmerized by our work."

Cindy then walked back towards me, took my hand and led me towards the back, where all the magic was done. As we were walking, Cindy said, "There's no more time to waste. Let's get started."

I believe Cindy was an evil genius. She thought it would be fun that during the entire process, I should be wearing a sleep mask. I was in total darkness. It reminded me of the games when we were kids trying to knock out piñatas. I was moved around, measuring tapes were violating every inch of my frame, making me more aware of some imperfections I had. Then I was put on a chair and my scalp was being roughed up like never before. They said that you had to suffer to be beautiful, well I figured that I was going to be freaking gorgeous by the end of this. I could feel the aluminum being added to my hair and that told me that I would have different colored hair, which scared me. There was no conversation being made to me. No small talk. They didn't care. They were just doing their jobs. Cindy would come from time to time asking if I was ok. I'd answer a shy yes and she'd go back to telling one of her workers how to do certain things. My nails were worked on, my work clothes were practically ripped off of me and I could feel the expensive dress being put on me. Where it was loose, I could feel them pull on it and hear them write on a piece of paper. The process was long and I was in total darkness. When done, there was no more aluminum in my hair and the dress was on me along with high heel shoes that I was not used to. Thanks to the help of Cindy, I presumed, I was able to walk along. We walked and walked and then stopped. The sleep mask was removed from my eyes and I was face to face with Simon.

There was dead silence in the room and I assumed in Simon's head. The look in his face was beyond flabbergasted. I wondered if it was a good thing or a bad thing. I searched to look for a mirror. As I made one step towards my right, I almost slipped. Simon caught me in time. I smiled and said, "Thank you."

He still didn't say anything. His face was still in that vegetable state. A full length mirror was brought to me by the LYD staff, but I didn't see me in there. The woman looking back at me was incredible. She was gorgeous. I was gorgeous.

My make up really brought out my hazelnut eyes and my hair looked like a milky chocolate waterfall with caramel highlights. My oval face was still showing and you could see my resemblance to Maria, although I was a lot darker.

The cleavage I displayed was very sexy without giving me the look of a high priced prostitute. But the alterations were not the only thing that made the dress look good. My shape was mostly at fault. My body looked like it could burst out of the dress. I was not petite like a model, but a little more built. All that training in high school paid off.

Simon's mouth opened, trying to utter some sort of sound.

I turned to him, smiling and asked, "Well?"

Simon still stayed there, with his dumbfounded expression, but the curves on his mouth showed the attempt of a smile, but something may have gone wrong. I said to him, "Simon, baby, can you snap out of it? You still have to pay this lady, remember?"

Finally, Simon said, almost like a machine, "You are the most beautiful woman I've ever laid eyes on."

I smiled. The compliment was more than appreciated because I could tell that he looked for it from the time I came out to see him. I said, "Thank you! Now please, go and pay the woman."

Simon flashed his signature smile. The Shark was back in control. He then walked towards the lady and gave his credit card. She walked away and Simon stood there, looking at me, almost in admiration. He looked proud.

Cindy came back and gave him back his card. She then said, "Thank you for shopping with us. It was a pleasure doing business with you, Mr. Smith."

Simon then took me by the hand and we both walked out to the limousine. We stepped in and I said, "I can't believe I walked into L.Y.D. and walked out with one of their product. Last time someone said that around my neighborhood, they had to steal it."

"Oh really?" asked Simon.

"Yeah, she told the whole story from jail over the phone," Simon chuckled. I smiled and asked, "Where are we off to now?"

Simon said, "We're headed to that newly opened French Restaurant at the Peninsula on 108 E Superior Street."

"Oh yeah, I heard of it," said I, "I forgot what it's called."

"I know what it's called. I just can't seem to pronounce it. The name means Craftsman of Flavor"

We were making our way to the restaurant called *L'Artisan De Saveur*. It was rumored that the owner started out as a small time waiter in some little joint in Montreal, Canada.

As Simon and I walked into the very prestigious restaurant, I suddenly felt really little, more little than I've ever felt in my entire life. Everyone in the restaurant, I knew, but none of them knew me. I had seen them over and over again, but they never paid attention to who I was.

All of Chicago's high class celebrities were there, whether popular in entertainment, politics or criminal activity. They were all there . . . Players from professional sports teams either dining with their wives, girlfriends or women they should not be having dinner with, or music industry moguls, not necessarily from Chicago, were there dining as well, talking business. Drug lords were there dining with political figures.

The restaurant had very bright lighting. Over thirty tables were being served, each table with its own light; each table cloth had golden trims on their; each table had its own waiter and light.

Before we were even brought to our table, Simon made sure to introduce me to the mayor of Chicago who had just finished having dinner with his wife. I felt like Cinderella. My fairy God Mother known as Cindy from LYD made me look the way I do while Simon was the one who used his magic wand or should I say credit card to make it happen.

After saying hi to the mayor, Simon took me by the hand and we followed the waiter to our table. As we sat down, I asked Simon, "How many times did you come here?"

"It's my first time here."

"Really? It seems like you been here more often."

"Not really . . . I've been told it was good by some friends, so I thought I'd take you on Valentine's Day," said Simon looking at the menu. He then asked me, "You think you'll be all right ordering? It seems like everything is in French here."

I looked at the menu and indeed, the French was quite overwhelming. I looked for words that I could understand with the VERY little French I learned from high school.

Everything on the menu might as well have been written in Chinese because I couldn't understand a thing, up until I read *Tête De Veau A La Fraise*. I remembered reading the word *Fraise* on the yogurts they sell at the convenience store. That meant Strawberry. I decided to order that. As per Simon, he pointed out to the waiter what he wanted. Once, the *Garçon* was gone, I asked Simon, "Do you know what you ordered?"

"Nope. You?"

I shook my head no and we both laughed.

A few minutes later, the waiter came with a huge plate and a smaller plate. Both plates were covered with a bell shaped silver plated cover, just like in the cartoons. At the site of that, I was already excited for what I had ordered. The aroma was incredible. I couldn't wait to eat. I could already taste the strawberries. The waiter placed the bigger plate in front of me and the other plate was placed in front of Simon. Before uncovering my meal, I looked over at Simon's plate and saw that he only had wings on his plate. Lucky guess.

I looked at my silver bell covered plate and couldn't help but be attracted by the aroma. I couldn't get any worse than Simon with something that smelled so good. That's what I thought. I uncovered my plate and held both my hands to my mouth to keep from screaming, although, muffled shrieks could be heard. I looked at Simon who was looking at my plate and couldn't help but mutter the words, "What.The.Fuck?"

The waiter who was able to catch my reaction walked himself to me and asked as he leaned towards me in a French and snobbish accent, "Is everything ok?"

Simon asked, "What did you give her?"

The waiter answered, "We gave her exactly what she wanted . . . Strawberry sprinkled head of veal."

I almost vomited and fainted at the same time. Simon himself looked repulsed to know that this restaurant would offer that type of thing. Simon, with a simple hand gesture, called the waiter to him. Simon whispered something to him as he slipped a $100 bill in the man's pocket. After which, the waiter picked up my plate. He later came along with a plate with tiny sausages and hot yellow sauce spread on the plate and little leafs decorating the meal.

The smell from the sauce was coming up strong. Almost like mustard. Simon said, "That's the Dijon sauce. Very popular in France."

I didn't really care. I was just happy I had some normal looking food on my plate.

As we were done eating, Simon smiled looking at me. I returned the smile. The moment was magical. We ate, we laughed. He explained the whole complexity of refined food and delicacies. He made me laugh, he made me happy. I wanted to give myself to him. I had decided to do it.

Simon then called the waiter at the table. As the waiter arrived, he asked him, "Excuse me, but I would like to know something here. What kind of seasoning did the cook use for this meal? The wings did not taste the same as I usually had it."

The waiter made a face which showed that something was wrong. The waiter then said to Simon, "It's not *wings* that you had sir. They were frog legs."

Simon's eyes widened as much as they could. He couldn't believe what he allowed to reach his mouth. He took a big sip of water and just gargled hoping that the remaining particles of the frogs inside his mouth would just leave. He then looked at the waiter and through sign language, he requested for some type of place for him to spit the contaminated water which was in his mouth. The waiter, who seemed to have understood, went under their table and picked up a bowl with a towel. Simon spit in it and the waiter gave him the towel after.

Me, in the meantime, couldn't help but laugh at the ordeal. I said as I took another bite of the tiny sausages, "That was too funny."

Simon looked at me, not pleased and said, "I'm glad this amuses you. Why don't you ask him how he cooked your sausages?"

At that time, the waiter made the same face which indicated that something was wrong. He then said, "Those were not sausages that were given to her."

About thirty minutes later, Simon and I arrived at his apartment. I searched for the bathroom desperately as soon as the front door opened. When I found it, I regurgitated the awful food I ate. I could hear Simon, laughing at me, saying, "That's what you get for laughing at me."

His phone then rang. I was still over the toilet, giving away the chunks of food mixed with the bitter taste of acidity that my stomach produced, when he came along, still laughing, saying, "Hey, Maria is on the phone."

I heard him say, "Yeah, she's in the bathroom, throwing up!"

He continued, "We had gone down to this French restaurant . . ."

He was still laughing, unable to control himself. I managed to raise my hand and flip him off as I fought the urge to throw up some more, a battle that I lost miserably.

"Sorry. Yeah, they gave her Pickled Orangutan Toes."

He laughed some more. Knowing Maria, she played stupid and acted like she didn't know what an Orangutan was. Simon, laughing, shouted, "She ate monkey toes!"

CHAPTER 9

Out Cold

Two weeks after the great French restaurant fiasco, I was back at Simon's condo. He offered to make it up to me by cooking for us. I made sure to supervise the entire preparation of the meal as I didn't want any surprises.

There were good things that happened that night though. I had decided to keep the hair style that was made for me by the ladies at LYD. I really enjoyed the attention I got from everyone when they saw it. I was not used to it, but I couldn't help but enjoy it. Not only did I like it, but Simon liked it too. Another big reason as to why I kept the hairdo.

While in his apartment, I realized that the other night, in my haste to vomit the other night, I didn't notice or appreciate the beauty of my boyfriend's dwelling. The numerous paintings depicting the black struggle from slavery to the pictures of various civil rights leaders and events were decorating his walls leading to the dwelling along as the living room.

I was happy that I had found the washroom when I did that night because I would've felt bad if I had thrown up on his beautiful white couches. I don't know the material, but it looked like some kind of fur on it. It felt very soft when I touched it. The couches were in a semi-circle shape and they were facing each other looking as though someone had split them down the middle. The space between them served as a trail leading to the kitchen door on the right side and to the bathroom on the left side. Behind the couch that was farthest from the door was two bedrooms; a small one for guests and the master bedroom for Simon.

The feast preparation was made with a lot of playful gestures in the kitchen like throwing food at one another. So much that we couldn't finish cooking and had to end the night ordering Chinese food.

We were in the living room, Simon sitting on the couch and I on the floor next to him, laughing at the crazy adventure we had at the French restaurant while.

Then, during a silent moment, Simon said, out of the blue, "I'm so lucky to have you in my life."

He then leaned over and kissed my lips. Not any type of kiss though. It was a sensuous, soft kiss. His lips touched mine, not too long so he didn't seem too eager and overly excited and not too fast so he didn't seem uninterested. It was just a sensual peck on my lips that gave me goose bumps.

As Simon was pulling back, I held him and pulled him towards me. And with me playing the role of the aggressor at that time, we both started to make out like a couple of young high school kids.

We kissed so much and so passionately, that our hands had to join in. Holding on to Simon's head, I sat on top of him and after a few seconds, I moved my pelvis against his crotch, doing dance moves that I had not practiced yet. From there, I felt his hands making their way to my top, unbuttoning every button in the clumsiest of ways, but with a determination to remove the obstacle.

As he was triumphant, he was faced with another obstacle in the form of my black lace bra protecting my bust. The same bra that Simon purchased for me the previous month as an ensemble, which let him know that I was definitely wearing the matching lace Brazilian underwear that came with it. And I could tell that it excited him even more. He started to kiss my chest, but didn't try to remove the bra. Every slobbery kiss that fell on my chest gave me a tingling feeling. I know I was turned on, but I felt this uncertainty as well though. Before I knew it, he had made his way to my pants, trying to remove them.

Right there, I saw how serious this game of pleasure was getting. I couldn't play. I was not ready. The uncertainty grew stronger as the lust became weaker. And Uncertainty was not fighting fair. It came along with Fear and the two beat down my lust.

I put my hands on top of his and held his hands as I removed myself from his lap. We were breathing very heavily. Simon was looking at me baffled as if he had walked in on the robbery of his greatest possession. He asked, "Is there something wrong?"

I said, "I'm sorry baby. I mean, I want you, but I can't do this yet."

Simon looked at his crotch and then at me, almost as though as if he was annoyed. Seeing that, I felt as though I may have made a mistake. Therefore, I kissed him and said, "Look, I'm sorry. I'm really sorry. I just can't do it. Please don't be mad at me."

Simon looked me in my eyes. His look went from annoyed to seeming indifferent. I became worried. His whole demeanor change. It was a side of him that I had never seen . . . I was scared. I mean, I knew that he had been patient and that's why I thought that maybe my non compliance to his needs was getting the best of him.

He then let out a big sigh and said, "Its ok."

He flashed his signature smile getting back to his old regular self that I learned to appreciate. He asked, "You want some wine?"

I was relieved in seeing that. I smiled back and kissed him again. I then said, "I hope you're not mad with me, *querido*. I mean, you understand, right?"

Simon still smiling kissed me back. He then got up and walked towards the kitchen. I sat there and started to think about my morals and what it is that I was doing. This guy was great to me. I mean, that's one compromise I should be able to do for him. He always went all out for me. I just couldn't go out like that though. I just couldn't! If I could get my head right around the idea, I probably would be comfortable enough to do it. Yeah, that's what I would do . . . But not tonight.

Simon then walked in with two wine glasses filled with red wine and sat back next to me. He smiled again and handed me a glass. I took it and smiled at him. As I took a sip from my glass, Simon placed his on the table in front of us. I asked him, "Are you still mad?"

Simon placed his hand on the back of my neck and as he rubbed me there, he said, "I was never upset baby. I was just really into it and when you stopped . . . I had to get back to myself."

I took another sip from my drink, but this time, the sip was bigger. I then said, "You know that I don't mean to be a tease, right?"

Simon nodded yes. I smiled and said, "Baby, you're very special to me and trust me, I'm getting there. But I can't do it just yet."

Simon leaned forward towards me again and kissed me the same way he did before, with a soft touch. Again, I was feeling the goose bumps, and went after Simon again. I started kissing him again, but after fifteen minutes of nonstop making out, I started to feel funny. My eyes started to feel heavy. I looked at Simon and he was still kissing on me. I tried to utter a few words, but couldn't. Then suddenly, everything went dark.

CHAPTER 10

True Colors

When I came to, I was feeling very groggy. Almost like a hangover, but not like it. I had a hangover before, partying with Maria, but this was not the same.

Unaware of my surroundings, I looked around me. As things in my head started to become less fuzzy, I realized that I was on a bed, but it was not mine. That bed was way too big and more comfortable. I concluded that I was not home. I kept looking around and found that Simon was next to me, sleeping. I started to smile, but then, as I was becoming more aware of the situation, I realized that I was not wearing any clothes. Fear gripped me. What happened? I lifted the sheets and my fears were confirmed. He was without clothing as well. I snapped out of my grogginess quickly and started to become hysterical.

What truly happened? Did I have sex with Simon? How could I when I knew that I was not approving? Was it the wine? Impossible! I drank wine many times and never found myself unable to control my actions.

Something was afoot. I slipped out of the bed, slowly. I didn't want to wake him up just yet. I had to find out what happened before I faced him. I then looked around the room for my clothes. Nothing was there.

I quietly stepped out of the room to get inside the living room, still naked. My eyes were accustomed to the darkness by now and I started on my scavenger hunt. I found my blue jeans on the floor in front of the bedroom door, with my panties and socks not too far away. My shoes were in front of the kitchen's entrance. I dressed myself up as I found my clothes. I walked inside the kitchen and found my bra and top on the counter. I put on my bra and then picked up my top. But under it, I found a small container, looked like it was medicine.

I picked it up to look at it closer. I then dropped it wanting to scream, but unable to do so. It was *Rohypnol* better known to the world as *Roofies.*

I now knew what had happened. I didn't want to believe it, but I knew. The wine, the knockout and the nakedness . . . It all made perfect sense.

Tears started flowing down my eyes. I sat on the kitchen floor, crying, not believing this had happened. I eventually was going to sleep with him, but he had to take it from me without my approval. Asshole!

Then I heard a noise coming from the other room. I quickly put on my top, and picked up the container of Roofies on the floor and quickly proceeded to make my way out of the premises, not before grabbing my coat.

Without looking back, I kept running, in the cold Chicago winter. As though my feet knew where to go, I just kept running without thinking. Not looking where I was going and not realizing that it was 6 o'clock in the morning, I was running. Afraid that Simon might be after me, trying to stop me, I just ran. Unable to stop the flood which had started flowing from my eyes, my face was drenched as though it had rained. I ran and felt the wind push me forward, helping me make it to my destination faster.

In the cold winter of the Windy City, I ran and at the end of my race, I found myself at my sister's apartment. Luckily for me, someone was actually stepping out the apartment building at the same time I was coming in. I didn't even bother waiting for the elevator. I just ran up the 10 flights of stairs of the high rise. When I reached apartment 1014, I started banging on the door, crying, screaming, "MARIA! MARIA!"

And I kept going like that for 5 minutes, until Maria, finally opened the door. Some of Maria's neighbors came out looking at what could be causing the commotion.

As she dragged me inside the apartment, Maria said, "Come in quick before you wake the entire building."

As Maria shut the door behind her, she looked at me. I was on my knees, crying and shivering from the cold, not even looking at her. She slowly came to me and held me in her arms. I grabbed onto her for dear life. I could guess that Maria saw that this was nothing usual. I was really hurt. Gently passing her hand through my damp hair, she asked, "What happened *querida*?"

I just burst out into tears and we stayed like this for a good 10 minutes, just letting my crying being our song as she rocked me in her arms. I couldn't talk until I knew that I was safe. I didn't want Simon bursting into the apartment. I didn't want to start talking until I knew that this was not a nightmare that I could wake up from.

Realizing that all of this was reality and that I was indeed safe in my sister's arms, I took the container of Rohypnol that I had and gave it to Maria. Maria looked at it and as a concerned looked appeared on her face, she asked, "Who the hell gave you this?"

I said, "Simon put that in my drink and I woke up in his bed, totally naked. While I was looking for my clothes, I found that in the kitchen."

Shock and anger now dressed Maria's face. Angrily, she asked, "What did that fucker tell you when you woke him up?"

"I didn't. I just left running."

Maria, shocked, asked, "You ran? From his place to mine? You ran?"

I nodded yes.

"Do you know how far his condo is from my place? Plus do you know how cold it is outside?"

I screamed, "Do you think I care? He raped me!"

Maria looked at me with pity in her eyes. Then she started to cry. And seeing her, I joined and we both cried like this. After another good 10 minutes, Maria said, wiping the tears off her eyes, "You don't have to worry about getting hurt like this ever again. You don't even have to worry about Simon. We will get him back. We will make him pay."

Like a baby, I held on to Maria and just started remembering a few years ago. Maria was 17 and I was 15. We were both in high school at the time and Maria was not the same girl.

Maria was an A student. She was not as boy crazy, but she was still dating. At that time, she was in love with a young man, Melvin Arthur Smith. He was the school's basketball star, and nominee for prom king.

I remembered that it was 2 weeks before prom night. Melvin and Maria were set to be the best looking couple at prom. I had never met or spoken to Melvin. Maria had convinced me to cut class with her to introduce me to her boyfriend.

But I recalled that as we walked the halls to meet her love interest, we stopped as we turned the corner because we saw Maria's boyfriend kissing another girl. That night, Maria was at home crying and mama was there reassuring her and telling her, "You don't have to worry about getting hurt like this ever again. You don't even have to worry about this Negro. We will get him back. We will make him pay."

I was remembering that it was from that day that Maria changed. It was from that day she changed her outlook on life.

I also remembered that from that day, she decided to never trust a man.

CHAPTER 11

Retribution

I woke up that morning in my bed. I sat up and looked at the ground, thinking about my day, thinking about what needed to get done. I then stood up and went into the bathroom.

I just stood there as the water started running. That was one of the only places where I was at peace considering that the past two weeks were a total nightmare. I just stood there, water running down my body and tears running down my cheeks. Images were flashing in my head, dark images of a man on top of me, like a raging animal, moving violently. The images were telling me a story, a story I knew the ending of, but hated. A story that I wished had never existed or was only a figment of my imagination, but somehow was only too real. I then snapped out of it and finished showering.

I then got out and walked into my room. There I laid down the grey business suit that Simon had bought me and a briefcase. I put it on and looked at myself in the mirror I had. There I had a little smile looking at myself. I did 2 or 3 pose in front of the mirror, as if I was shooting for Elle Magazine, like a little high school girl would do. I was enjoying that look, but then, my smile changed to a serious look, a determined look. I put my hair in a ponytail and looked again. I was ready to face what that day had to offer.

From the time I walked out of my room until I reached outside, it was the same look on my face. People were stepping out of my way as though they knew I was a force to be reckoned with. It was as though they feared to be at the receiving end of my wrath. They knew I was going out looking for blood.

The wind accompanied me. It knew that I was going for vengeance, but that day, the wind was approving of my actions. It was going to help me achieve my desired goal.

I had two weeks to sort out all of my feelings. I was looking to go out indifferent, but the only feeling that stayed was anger. I was mad. Retribution would be mine. I was going to get my dues today.

I finally reached my destination. It was a little phone booth in the midst of Downtown Chicago. I went in and dialed.

"Hello?"

Silence on my end of the phone.

"Hello?"

It reminded me of that first day when I called Simon for the first time. He kept saying *Hello? Hello?* And I stayed quiet then because of nerves. I stayed quiet now, because I was trying to not blow a gasket.

I then heard, "Fine, if you don't want to talk."

I finally let out, "We have to talk."

Simon's voice changed. He was sounding more sincere as he said, "Baby . . . I've been looking for you for the past 2 weeks. What happened?"

I said again, in a more stern voice, "We have to talk!"

Simon paused. He then asked, "Where are you?"

I said, "Look outside your window. I'm at the payphone by the coffee shop."

I looked up at the building and at the 6th floor, I saw him looking down and although we were far from each other, we locked eyes.

Simon asked, "How come you're not coming upstairs?"

I said, "Come and meet me inside the coffee shop. We have to talk!"

Simon said, "I'm kind of busy here . . . Can it . . ."

"Now!" I shouted.

I then hung up.

I walked inside the coffee shop which was on the same street corner as the phone booth. I ordered a French Vanilla and sat at the table in the middle of the establishment. Without taking a sip of my coffee, I just sat there, watching the front door. It took about 5 minutes after having ordered my coffee before Simon walked in. He was wearing a black suit, with an open white shirt inside and a black t-shirt on the inside.

When he walked in, he flashed his smile, like the shark he was, and walked towards me. He leaned towards me to plant his magic kiss on my lips, but little did he know that the magic was gone. Instead, all he received was a cold stare. People often say *if looks could kill* . . . Well, if looks could kill, my look would have been the start and the end of a new World War. The shortest global conflict, but the most devastating.

Simon knew not to expect a walk in the park after seeing my response. He sat down in front of me and said, "I've been worried about you. Your mother said she didn't know where you were and your sister wouldn't pick up her phone. Linda, at your job, said that you called in sick."

Still with that cold stare on my face, I said, "I've been staying at Maria's apartment. I went back to my mother's house last night. I was going to come a week earlier, but something happened. That's why we need to talk now."

Simon, trying to act dumb, asked, "Can't I order something first?"

I said, "No you can't! If you order coffee, then you'll be comfortable. I don't want to give you that luxury."

I then took a sip of my French Vanilla which had cooled down and continued, "I should've had 5-0 called on your ass for what you did to me Simon. But I have a problem with cops. Get what I'm sayin?"

Simon nodded.

"You had the nerve . . . The balls to . . . to . . . to . . ."

Tears started to flow from my eyes, but it was no more pain or sadness that came flowing down. This time, anger and rage had set in. I took a deep breath and said, looking his eyes, "How dare you rape me?"

Simon said, looking to his left, "Now, don't . . ."

"LOOK AT ME!"

He looked around the coffee shop, to see who had become the spectator to our drama. I didn't care. I wanted to him to look me in the eyes when he answered. He said, leaning forward and using a tone above a whisper, "Can you please lower your voice down? Don't be using the word rape. You were willing to do anything I asked."

I shouted, "After you slipped drugs in my fucking drink, *Pendejo*!"

The coffee shop now started paying attention to me and Simon. Simon leaned towards me again and whispered, "Keep your voice down. We don't need everyone knowing about our business."

A smirk appeared on my face as I scoffed at his remark.

"When I left your place, I couldn't really remember what had happened, so I was asking myself if it really went down like that, but then I started having flashbacks, remembering bits and pieces of what went down. At first, it was all nightmares that I kept having. I can see you on top of me like a disgusting thing. I can't even describe you as human! Just disgusting!"

My face showed how repulsed I was by the images. Simon looked at me as I talked and I'm sure he could see the tears flowing down my eyes, but I never realized they were there. I became used to the whole crying thing. I still wiped them off my face.

I continued, "I wanted to make you pay Simon. My sister and I had come up with a plan to make you pay dearly for what you did to me!"

"Can't we work it out?"

"No. You took that option away when you did what you did to me."

I took another sip.

"Last week, I went to my doctor for a physical cause I wanted to make sure your dirty ass didn't give me anything and I found something."

Simon said, "I ain't got nothing! I'm clean!"

I laughed a little, "You're so fucking stupid!"

My little smirk then went away from my face and I went back to looking serious again.

"I'm pregnant."

Simon was now the one smiling. He started clapping and said, "Impressive! You wanted to pull a Robin Givens on me? Nice! Make me marry you with a fake pregnancy, then divorce me for half my shit! Real nice baby!"

Marry him? He really was a dumbass. I started digging inside my briefcase and said, "You truly are the dumbest fuck there is out there! I wouldn't want to be stuck in holy matrimony with a bitch like you!"

I finally found what I was looking for. I took out a stack of papers and handed them to Simon. Simon started reading and his smile went away from his face. He looked at my face. He was searching desperately for a sign that showed that I was bluffing. He should've known that I never bluffed. He looked and looked, but couldn't find the loophole he was looking for in his papers. He finally asked, "Why would you want to keep a child from a man who you claim "raped" you?"

"Pendejo! Hijo de la grande puta si no fura por que tu me viólate yo no tu viera que tiñera este hijo y tener que dicer le que su papa me violo."[19]

Simon said, "Whoa! Whoa! Chill! English please!"

I paused and took a deep breath again. I was holding everything in me from getting up and whooping his ass. I wanted to have my hand around his throat. I wanted to squeeze. I wanted to punch and kick him. Then, I thought about the past again. I couldn't do that again. It wouldn't happen again. I snapped out of my thoughts and said, "I don't believe in abortion, no matter the circumstances in which I got the child."

Simon looked at me upset and asked, "What do you want from me?"

I said, "Messing with you, I fucked up my education. Not entirely your fault. Mostly mine because I wasn't serious enough with mine! But I will make sure that you help me every step of the way for this child! Don't even think about trying to step out on that responsibility!"

Simon, getting more upset at the situation, let out, "I can't believe this shit!"

After seeing Simon angry and upset made, I smile a little more. I didn't get my retribution yet, but I knew that the child would make him suffer for what he did to me. He had not gotten his way and he was livid. I decided to rub it in a little more.

I took the documents from his hands and put them back in my briefcase. I then got up and said, "You know, I was thinking about baby names for this child. If it's a girl, I want to call her Simone. What do you think?"

Simon, not amused, snarled at me. It almost sounded like a growl. Hearing it, I laughed as loud as I could while making my way out the coffee shop, leaving Simon there with his thoughts and preparing myself to battle mine.

---

[19] Motherfucker! If you had not raped me in the first place, I wouldn't have to go through this.

CHAPTER 12

Never Again

Another nightmare.

Another night interrupted with evil images in my head, keeping me from going to sleep.

I touched my face and found more traces of tears that dried up.

I sat up at the edge of my bed looking down at the floor, trying to get my mind right, but then my stomach was starting to act up. I ran to the wash room and regurgitated whatever fluid that was left in my body.

This was the worst routine I had to experience in my entire life.

Once done, I always cried. I made what could possibly be the worst decision in my entire life. I did it on my own though . . . Actually, Maria helped.

Telling him was not an option. And having mama involved would be more than a problem.

It was the right decision. That way, I would not have to quit school.

But if it was the right decision, why was my heart breaking so much?

Making such a decision seemed to be easy when I thought of all the consequences if I had not gone through with it.

But no one told me that I would be haunted with all these nightmares. No one told me that I would feel so much pain. And why was the pain there?

I thought about it since the day that it was done. I was empty. I was void. I had taken out a part of me that I wished I had kept.

I cried some more, as I sat next to the toilet. I was a horrible person. Regardless of what had happened, I shouldn't have gone through with this.

I regretted my decision with everything in me. Even if mama was ready to kick me out, he would've taken me in with him, in his house.

I stood up and flushed the bile that had filled the commode. I caught a glimpse of myself in the mirror. How I wanted to punch myself out. How I wanted to be able to go after my reflection and give it a piece of my mind. But then after a while, it looked like the reflection was the one mad at me and that I should fear its wrath.

After feeling much kind of pains in my life, this experience made me realize that you get used to the physical pain. It hurts, but it does not last that long.

It's the emotional pain that really takes you out. The pain from the heart right where the love resides is a pain that doesn't go away. It goes through your flesh, flows into your veins, throughout your entire body to get straight to the heart and stays to a point where it controls your breathing.

From that moment on, I swore and promised myself that I would never again have another abortion. The feeling of taking a life was too much for me.

I also swore and promised myself that Cooper would never know that he could have been a father at 17 years of age.

CHAPTER 13

The Verdict

I packed up my bags. Everything that I owned in my room was already in boxes. I was ready for the move.

I had found the number of a storage company that could help me hold on to my stuff for a little while.

Now, what did I need to do next? Nothing. I just had to go and face mama, like Maria offered for us to do.

Maria said that Mama would not get mad and that I was over estimating the situation.

I got pregnant and I was keeping it . . . this time. How was that over estimating the situation? I was positive that Mama was going to kick me out. I was positive that she was going to scold me into dust.

"*Dolores! Tenemos que dejar ahora*[20]!"

Her voice scared the hell out of me. I took a deep breath rethinking the whole plan. I tried calming down, reassuring myself that it will go well.

"Dolores!"

With my attempts to be calm disrupted, I just rushed out the door hoping for the best.

We walked about 25 minutes to Oakton so we could catch the 97. I looked down the entire time. I was already showing signs of guilt, but mama was not commenting. I wish we didn't have to do this, but Maria

[20] Dolores! We have to leave now!

said it would be best if we met her in a public setting and spoke to her there.

The worst part was that I had to travel with Mama to that place and being in an awkward silence with her for 1 hour and 30 minutes was just as agonizing as sitting across from her waiting for an inevitable response.

The next hour in the bus and subway was not that peaceful. Mama would look at me from time to time. She'd look at me intensively as if she was trying to read me, but I did my best to engage my environment. Reading every commercialized message on the bus, whether sponsored by some company or advertised by some disgruntled rider who felt the need to express themselves with the help of a permanent marker.

I looked at every man who dared to look at me and looked them straight in the eyes. They'd either look down or away. That was something I saw Maria doing. She said that it was fun for her. I did the same with the women and they'd look away as well.

I needed entertainment and something to keep my mind off of the impending confrontation that was coming my way. I didn't want to start anything with my mother right then either.

We traveled from Howard Terminal until the Chicago Terminal and walked to Del-Iberico. We stayed quiet, even as we sat in the high wooden chairs, having bottles of wine resting above us, right before we ordered drinks. It seemed like the entire Latin community of Chicago was attending the deli. I could not even make out a word of English, except for when the waitress came to take our orders. As soon as the waitress took our orders and left, mama asked, "*Qué es todo el secreto acerca de?*[21]"

I looked at her, my heart pounding harder than anything I've ever hit. I looked at her frozen in time. Just like in the movies, movements in the restaurants were in slow motion. It surprised me for a moment, but then I knew why it was happening. Time had decided to wait on me to respond to her and tell her why she had come.

As the words flowed out of my mouth, time had decided to go back to its usual pace, "*Estoy embarazada.*[22]"

I sat there and looked at her, my heart still pounding. I thought that my revealing my secret would end the pounding, but my heart kept playing the music, waiting for her to react to what I said.

---

[21] So what is all the secrecy about?

[22] I'm pregnant

She looked at me, with a relaxed look on her face. No anger, no sadness, no disappointment. She asked, "*Quien es el padre*[23]?"

I looked down, scared to answer. Still looking down, I just said, "Simon."

"*Que pasa con la educación*[24]?"

A chill went through me as I heard that question. I looked at her, forgetting that she could ask me about that. I realized that the answer to that question was going to ensure my fate. I answered, looking back down, "I flunked all my classes. I can't go back."

I stayed there looking down waiting for my sentence to be given to me, but not a word was uttered; as though my judge, jury and executor were still deliberating. I finally looked up so I could see the reaction. She was just sitting there, nodding. Her lack of reactions scared me more than her exploding at me. I could hear the words, *get out of my house,* being said to me in English, Spanish and if my mother could find a way, she'd probably try it in French and Russian.

She just sat there though, still looking at me and then let out a sigh as though she was exhausted and fed up. After that, she started. She spoke of how irresponsible I was. She said that she always told me that this would happen. She blamed my genes, saying that had traces of my father all over. She spoke and spoke. She never stopped talking and condemning my actions. Even when the waitress came around with our drinks, she would not stop.

Mama did not stop talking, even when Maria came around, she was able to get out of the conversation, greet her and get back into it. Just constantly nagging. But in all the nagging, I never heard her utter the words, *get out of my house.*

---

23 Who's the father?

24 What about your education?

CHAPTER 14

Betrayal

The 72 bus was filled with a bunch of people that day, when I got in. Looking around, for a little while, I wondered what these people could be thinking about. Who had a broken heart? Who had to worry about payments to get paid? Who was rushing to meet a loved one? Considering that the year before, they all thought that we were going to go back to the dark ages . . . New millennium my ass. People bought supplies because the year 2000 was supposed to bring an immediate crash to all electronics. That had been the popular topic of conversation among folks and a year later; it was the topic of jokes for all comedians.

But then again, I had my own problems to worry about and so I forgot about everyone else and started looking for a place to sit.

It looked like I would be standing holding on to the little one. It was only a little while ago that she turned 1 year old.

The good thing about travelling with your child, I thought, was that undesirable men would not attempt to play Casanova around me. Instead, I got the attention from older folks, if they had not already jumped to the conclusion that I was a mother that had slept around one time too many. The usual question would be, *what's her name? How hold is she?* Followed by comments such as *She's so precious! Look at the cute little girl!*

That day, I was on that bus standing with my baby in my arms. I could've been with a stroller, but to get it in the bus and then get it out was too much of a hassle for me. Plus I liked holding on to my daughter like that. It made me feel closer to her.

As we made our way to the back of the bus, I saw Mr. Samuels sitting there, looking at us with a smile on his face, almost proud, it seemed. He then asked, "Would you mind sitting down?"

Seeing him straightening up with the help of his cane, I started to feel bad for the handicapped gentleman. I said, "No, we're ok! You stay seated and rest, Mr. Samuels."

The old man responded, as he stood up, "I ain't that old sweetheart!"

He then pointed towards the seat with his cane and I looked at him with a smile. I then said, "You're sweet."

Only because he had insisted, I sat down.

As I did so, my daughter then started to lift her hands towards the elderly man, as though she knew him. Mr. Samuels asked, "Is that the child I've been hearing about all this time?"

I smiled looking at my baby and said, "Yes, sir. That is Shannon."

I never had any intentions of calling her Simone. I had realized that I could've gotten an abortion considering the way she was conceived. But I couldn't bring myself to taking another life.

The most beautiful aspect of the whole thing was that Shannon was born on Christmas day, as though it was a confirmation that she was meant to be mine.

The bus stopped and the old man said, "That's my stop."

I said to my little girl, "Say bye to the nice man Shannon."

The old man said, looking directly in my eyes, "*Hasta la juego mi hija.*"

He then walked out. I didn't know Mr. Samuels spoke Spanish, but it gave me a warm feeling in my heart hearing those words.

Funny enough, when mama found out about my pregnancy, she didn't throw me out the house. Instead, she extended a helping hand; accompanied by comments such as, *always irresponsible, now look at you.*

She went to Lamaze classes with me when Maria couldn't make it. She was there in the delivery room with me when I pushed her out. She was actually holding on to the child more than I was. If she could, I bet she'd breast feed her too, so whenever I had to go to work, I had no problem finding a babysitter. My mother was the lady for it.

Once the child was born, Esperanza couldn't be happier, as though she loved being a grandmother, but she never stopped being hard on me.

To me, it was not a problem. The love I couldn't get from mama, I would give to Shannon. Every time I needed to talk to someone, I would talk to Shannon. All my insecurities, my pain and sorrows, I shared with Shannon. She probably didn't understand, but she was there and it seemed like she was paying attention and I liked it.

Maria was too busy hustling the hustlers on the streets. She was hard to get a hold of. I had no intentions on going to her apartment every night to see if my sister can be there for me. Therefore, I was happy that I had Shannon.

My relationship with Simon deteriorated from the time I called him into the coffee shop . . . What am I saying? Our relationship deteriorated from the time he got the *roofies*. He wasn't even present when the baby was born. He made sure he had not contact with the child as possible, but I made sure that my child saw her father. I didn't want Shannon to be like me, not knowing who my father was. Even if he didn't want to have anything to do with his child, Shannon would see him.

I wondered if things were as bad for my mother. Was the reason my mother and father didn't stay together similar to what I was experiencing with Simon? Did my father hate me as much as Simon hated my child? I tried not to compare the two as I could feel my heart breaking.

To make things worse for Simon, his business was not doing too good as he was getting investigated by the city on his activities outside the club. Rumors came out that he was involved with gangsters and drug dealers. His club started losing clientele and his money was not as flamboyant as he used to let it be shown earlier in our relationship. As that started happening, he started to despise our child even more. He actually believed that Shannon was the source of his misfortune, like a voodoo curse.

It was more like the Renee curse, cause I would *cuss* his ass out every time he was late on his child support payments. He showed that his money was the most important thing to him and Simon being forced to share that with anyone else made him very irate.

My trip continued as the bus stopped at the subway station on North Halsted & West North Avenue. There, I had to ride the train to West Grand Avenue for about 9-10 minutes. Funny enough, all Shannon did was look around her as she stayed still in my arms. She didn't cry or fuss like most kids did. I liked to think that she was more mature like that. When the subway arrived on Grand Avenue, I walked and made my way to Grand & Fairbank, Simon's condo.

He had been missing for 3 months and dodging my calls. That day, I was on a mission to get that money for Shannon.

Finally, we arrived at 600 N. Fairbanks. As we made our way through the halls of the condominium apartment, I was talking to my baby saying, "You can see how much of a trifling nobody your daddy is, dodging my calls and making me travel all the way here. That's the type of man you have to keep away from, a punk who's ready to make a baby, but won't take care of it."

The young child just kept saying, "Dada!"

I looked at her sadden by the harsh reality of her situation. I said, "I wish you could understand what's going on here, baby. You love your daddy so much, but yet, he don't want nothing to do with you."

Anyone looking on the outside would say that I was wrong for talking to my child like such, but Simon's actions towards the child were deplorable. He couldn't care less about the image that was portrayed about him to his child, nor did I care about how Shannon saw him.

Finally we reached the door to Simon's apartment, number 1501. I put Shannon down and held her hand. I then knocked on the door. There was no response. I knocked again. No one answered. I then saw my little girl trying to reach the doorknob. The baby was struggling; staying on her tippy toes, but couldn't reach the prize. I said, "You think the door is opened little one?"

The baby, as if she never heard me, was still trying to open that door. I, therefore, turned the knob. The door opened. It looked like Simon had forgotten to lock down his place.

Too bad that was the case though. I would've been spared the horrific sight that I happened to witness. Right there on his couch, Simon was laying with a woman on top of him. Thrusting her pelvis on his harden genitals.

I was not jealous. I was hurt though. I was hurt because the woman on top of Simon was Maria. I couldn't care less for Simon to be with any woman he wished to be with, but not my sister. Maria could fuck the entire world for all I care, but not my enemy.

I was in a state of shock as I saw this, but Shannon thought her father was playing a game with her aunt. Therefore, she ran towards them screaming, "Dada! Dada!"

Simon, upset that the sex he was getting was being disturbed, shouted, "What the fuck is this?"

I just stood there looking at Maria, who in turn did the same. Our eyes just locked and it looked as if we were the only ones in the room for that moment. No words between us, just silence, but outside of our trance, Simon and Shannon were as loud as they could be. It was as though the level of communication had transcended to a form of telepathy between the two of us. Me asking Maria, *How could you?*

And Maria was just too ashamed to even answer. After what seemed an eternity, I just broke out of the trance and broke our telepathic link and walked out of the apartment. I wanted nothing to do with the mess that was going on in there. I just wished to leave it all behind.

Then, my arm was grabbed and I was pulled backwards, finding myself, face to face with an angry Simon in his boxers. Holding a crying Shannon with the other hand, he shouted out, "You're not leaving here without this goddamn child!"

Tears ran down my face as my anger started to rise. I wanted to hit him. I wanted to hurt him. And then I wondered, *Why wanting to hit him when I can just do it?*

So I kneed him in his privates. Simon's angry face was erased by a look of pain as he went down, releasing both Shannon and me. As he was on his knees gasping for air, I punched the father of my child in his face. Simon was completely laid out on the ground at this time.

I stood over his body, still angry and still wanting to hurt him more. So I went to work, kicking him over and over again. It was not too long for Simon's blood to come out and start staining my cream shoes I had bought at payless a few weeks ago.

But the punishment that I had started to unleash on the Shark soon came to an end as Maria stepped out of the apartment, fully clothed.

She tried to look at me, whilst tears ran down her cheeks and see if she could find a little bit of love in my eyes, but she was unsuccessful. Her act had stained the entire relationship both of us had, much like Simon's blood had done with my shoes, although we already were not that close to begin with.

So she whispered *I'm sorry* as she gave me an envelope.

I looked inside and found money, a lot of money. Passing right by me, all I heard was the sound the heel of her shoes were making. As soon as she was 2 steps behind me, I started, without turning around, "You know . . ."

The heel had stopped. Maria had stopped moving. She had not turned around either. I don't think she did.

With our backs facing each other, I continued, "I never judged your lifestyle. Cause after what Melvin did to you, I figured that if you had to do dirt on all these men, they had it coming. But I always thought you had a limit on the people you had to hurt. I thought your family was that limit."

Maria took a deep breath. Our backs were still conversing, as though it was no longer permitted for us to look at one another. Maria said, "That was all business, *querida*."

I finally heard her heels going and the sound fading until I heard nothing again.

I fought the urge to cry as I picked up Shannon and made my way out. But as I did, I didn't just leave Simon on the ground, along with that envelope of money Maria had given me. I left so many more things as well. Whatever relationship I had with Maria was left there in that sinful place along with my willingness to let people walk all over me. I couldn't take that money knowing how she had gotten it and where it came from.

I decided to change from that time on. From that day, I swore that I would never allow neither man, nor woman to break my heart without making them suffer for it. And if I was asked why, I would just say, *it's all business!*

CHAPTER 15

Exits The Shark . . . Enters The King

My Addiction was closed. In front of the building, a note was posted on the front doors stating that the business had been closed due to non-payment of rent and that it would not reopen until the amount of $50,000 was paid by the previous tenant or until a new business came about.

No one was able to find Simon. Speculations were that he had fled the country. I liked to think of it in a mythological way. The great black shark was defeated and could not face his opponent again. Not that there has ever been anything written about a great black shark running from his opponent, but I liked to see it like such.

When I thought of him, Maria also came to mind. She also disappeared. Maybe she ran off with Simon. I couldn't care less to say the truth. Only mama knew where she was. I could've asked her on many occasions and she would not have withheld the information from me, but I thought it was best that way. Staying away from Maria and Simon was the best thing for me.

As for myself, I only cared for the education and wellbeing of my daughter. The outside world did not matter. I didn't need a man or a friend. What I had with my daughter was the only relationship I needed to maintain.

Still living at home, my mother had a relationship with Shannon that I almost wished I could've had growing up. Mama would read to her, tell her stories about the old country or take her out to the park.

When I was younger, Mama read to me report cards or bills that came along. She would tell me stories of how awful a man my father was. She took me to the store with her when she needed help carrying bags.

I don't think that I was jealous. I just wished that I had a better childhood.

Nonetheless, I loved my daughter more than anything. Shannon was the joy of my life and making her the happiest little girl was my goal, without having to worry about a man.

Somehow though, I did wish I had another chance at romance, especially after seeing couples coming in and out of the convenience store, just wishing that I could have that man who would want to just give me love because I deserved it. Was that too much to ask?

That day was my 27th birthday, March 24th. It was almost two months after the CIA admitted that there was no imminent threat of weapons of mass destruction in Iraq. Funny how after that stunt in Iraq, Bush reminded me so much of Simon. That awarded the president a special place on my shit list. I, on the other hand, was awarded the title of store manager for my many years of dedication to the franchise. I was not dedicated. It was the one place I felt safe from my mama and anything else. I couldn't work anywhere else.

As I looked outside of my empty store, a man was walking by, looking like he was about to make his way in, but then was hailed by a police car. I looked on as two cops stepped out of the vehicle.

They talked to the pedestrian a little bit. One was black and tall, wearing sunglasses while the other one was a white man of medium height, shorter than the man who had been stopped. That cop also wore sunglasses. The tall cop was right in front of the pedestrian while the other one was behind him. The pedestrian's lips started moving real fast, while holding a very defensive stance. I assumed it was an argument. Finally, my show was ended when the man was forced inside the police car. I wondered what the issue could possibly have been about. The weirdest thing about this situation was that the cops didn't put handcuffs on him.

I could be the witness to the events that led to the murder of another Chicago citizen. I imagined the headlines on TV, about a man found dead in the Chicago River with a request for witnesses to come forward and I would, of course, provide them with the lead story that would help them catch the crooked cops. I would . . .

"Hello."

I jumped screaming.

Mr. Samuels jumped back just as scared as I was, his hat falling to the ground. My hand on my chest, I felt the beating of my heart going faster than I had before. I thought that this could've been one of the cops trying to get rid of any loose ends, meaning me.

Mr. Samuels asked picking up his hat, "What is it?"

With my hand still on my chest, I said, "I'm sorry. You startled me."

He straightened himself and then looked at me with a smile. I smiled back. I knew what to expect. He said, "It's a good day today. Isn't it?"

"Mr. Samuels, you know very well that it's my birthday today."

Mr. Samuels always made sure to bring me some sort of gift for my birthday from the very first year I started here. That first time, when he brought me a Teddy Bear, he told me that a little birdie told him about my birthday. I assumed one of the girls did and I never asked either. I was just glad I got a bear that year instead of the usual $20 I got from mama or whatever sex paraphernalia provided by Maria.

But this year, I didn't see anything in his hand. An empty handed Mr. Samuels came to my shop on my birthday. I was a little disappointed.

He said, as he placed the items he wanted to buy on the counter, "Well . . . Happy birthday."

I tabulated the whole thing and charged him $8 in total, with an insincere smile that usually other customers would get, but he failed to make me happy on my special day, so he got the same treatment they got. The man gave his money and started to make his way outside the convenience store. I looked at the bills he gave me and saw that he had given me an extra $100 bill. I screamed out before he made it outside, "Mr. Samuels! You gave me too much money!"

He said continuing to walk away, "Call it a gift! Happy birthday!"

I smiled at Mr. Samuels' act of kindness. He still came through on my birthday. I was glad that he was in my life. I decided that I would buy myself a phone with that money. My birthday present.

A couple of hours later, I was alone again, still at the counter, reading a magazine this time. Apart from enjoying the skills of Ms Alicia Keys singing about a young man she admired but who didn't know her name, I was living in complete boredom.

That was until a man walked in, not looking in the best of ways. He looked like he was 2 weeks overdue for a shave. His hair which was coming out of his dirty Chicago Cubs hat seemed uncombed and nappy. His clothes were baggy and not ironed and his shoes could've been mistaken for road kill. His ashy hands looked like they could use some cream or spit or something. The only thing he had going for himself was his skin tone, a nice brown chocolate color. And then after looking at him, I recognized him. I knew who he was. He was the guy that was taken by the cops a little while before. I knew that there was something wrong, considering that he was forced inside the cruiser, but not arrested.

The young man dropped 2 cans of Red Bull on the counter. I saw a ring on his right middle finger. The ring had a green stone and a golden K inside. The man was smiling like he had no worries in this world. I tried to see if there were signs of him being beaten up or if he showed signs of pain in his face. He looked happier than ever despite his dirty look. I thought he might be a bum who found himself some good fortune with a generous bystander and he was brave enough to step into the store.

I returned the smile to him and asked, "Found everything ok today sir?"

The man said, "Please, call me Richard."

I looked at him and asked, "Richard?"

"Yeah, everybody really calls me King Richard though."

I chuckled at the silliness and shook my head. I then asked smiling and sarcastically, "And I'm privileged enough to address his majesty as though we were in the same social status?"

Richard smiled and took my hand saying, "A King is capable of recognizing when he's in the presence of royalty."

My smile diminished as I understood what was going down right at that moment. I told myself that I was not going to be falling for no wannabe smooth bullshit line. No matter how original he tried to be. Plus his look was not helping his situation.

I said to him, removing my hand from his hold, "Nice try, but I saw that smooth shit a mile away. Not interested."

I then punched in a few buttons in the cash register and said to him, "It will be $5.39 for the Red Bull."

Richard nodded looking at me and then said giving me a $10 bill, "You probably don't pay attention, but I be walking by here many times still."

Counting his change, I said, "That's nice."

I then gave him his $4.61 change. Richard put the change in his pocket and just stood there. After a couple of seconds went by, I asked, "Is there anything else?"

Richard replied, "I don't think we should end this without dealing with our unresolved feelings here."

I smiled and said, "Spell unresolved."

Shocked, Richard stood there, with his mouth half opened. His majesty looked left and then right as if to see if someone was around, I looked as well and couldn't see anyone. Our eyes locked and he asked, "Why do you have to be so cold?"

"Why can't you get out of my face?"

"Cause you're too hot! I can't seem to get you out my head and I want to take you out to see if it was meant to be or not!"

"Why do you even want to go out with me? You don't even know my name."

"I know your name. You're Renee."

I looked at him shocked. I then asked, "How did you know my name?"

He pointed at my name tag. I looked and chuckled. I really was not interested in his character. What I was interested in was what went down with him and the cops earlier. I said, "Look, I'm flattered! I really am, but I had a bad breakup with my ex and it's hard for me to get into anything with anyone else right now."

"I believe I was sent to change that for you."

He was getting cornier and that was getting annoying. But my curiosity was still there. What happened once he got inside the cruiser? Where did they take him? No, I didn't need to know that badly.

"I don't want you to change anything! Now I'm going to need you to leave."

Richard looked around him again and said, "You know what? I know what I can do to make you say yes to 1 date."

The balls on this dude. With a look of complete disbelief, I asked, "Oh really? What's that?"

Richard took a step back and looked at me with a smile. He then took a deep breath and started singing,

And I am telling you . . .

I rolled my eyes to the ceiling and let out a "*Dios mió*!"

I'm not going. / You're the best woman I'll ever know. / There's no way I can ever go, / No, no, no, no way, / No, no, no, no way I'm livin' without you. / I'm not livin' without you. / I don't want to be freeeee. / I'm staaayin', / I'm staaayin', / And you,

"I got it!" I said. He continued, a*nd you . . .*

I screamed, "I SAID I GOT IT!"

You're gonna love meeeeeee. / Ooh, you're gonna love meeeee.

The man was off key but kept on going. Customers were walking into the store and that alarmed me as I didn't want to lose business because of such an indiscretion. I screamed out, "Stop! Stop singing now!"

Richard stopped and looked at me. He then asked, "We're going out?"

Why was he so persistent? I could call the cops, but it was not worth it. He didn't attack me. He serenaded me! Again, his look was nothing too hot for me. But I was curious about what happened earlier. I decided to attribute it to my curiosity.

I asked, "One date?"

"One date to make you fall in love with me and then if I fail, I'll get out of your hair."

I smiled and then said, "All right! One date and after that, you leave me alone."

Richard smiled and said, "I'll meet up with you right here tomorrow night @ 8 pm."

I said, "Good. That's the time I finish."

Richard walked towards the door with a big smile on his face and as he was about to step out, he said, "Trust me, we're going to be great together!"

He then stepped outside. The customers that walked in were an old couple who pretended to walk around as though they hadn't notice anything. I didn't mind.

Three seconds later, Richard poked his head back in the store and said, "*Hasta la vista!*"

I smiled as he stepped out. He then poked his head in again and said, "*Hasta la juego!*"

I crossed my arms on my chest as he stepped out again, but I looked at the door though, thinking that he'd make another appearance. When I thought that he was not going to come back in, I turned and to my surprise, he poked his head in again and said, "Hasta la mananana!"

I laughed and said, "You saying it wrong! It's *Hasta mañana*!"

He said, "See how you complete me!"

I smiled as he stepped out for the final time. I knew it was because I heard him shouting, "SHE SAID YES! I'M GOING OUT WITH HER!"

The old couple came to the counter and to try and save face, I lied, "He likes to overreact at certain times."

They smiled nervously and I went on about my business.

The next day, approximately around 8:15 pm, I was outside the convenience store waiting for his majesty, new cellular phone in my pocket; my very first one. I was just there with the city, taking it all in, enjoying the only time of peace and quiet I could get, outside of my shower.

The city at night was a great time for me to just let go and be free with my thoughts. I just enjoyed being there feeling the wind blowing by me. The wind and I were having our own little intimate moment. The far away police sirens could be heard, but it didn't faze me as it was part of the environment. That was Chicago singing its song to us. It was part of the love the wind and I shared.

But that moment could only last for a little while. The cold interrupted my romantic time with the city and I looked at my watch only to see that it was 8:25 pm. I got stood up! I mean, I really didn't mind since I never wanted to go on the date with him in the first place, but it was still insulting.

Luckily enough, a bus stop was a few feet away from me and a bus was coming. I made my way to the stop and as I reached, the bus arrived, opened its doors and King Richard stepped out looking totally different from the last time I saw him. His clothes were still baggy, but ironed and clean. His shoes actually looked somewhat nice, if anyone knew what brand was *Sprong*. This time, he was not wearing any hat and he looked like he had been at the barbershop, with a nice line up and chin strap goatee. He looked taller than the first time he walked into the store.

I wondered if he was taller than Simon. He asked me, "Where were you going?"

I answered, making my discontent heard, "You're late!"

"Not my fault! The damn buses don't run on the regular downtown!"

"You ask me out and you don't have a car?"

"So?"

"*Dios Mio*! You got balls man! You just lost major points on that one, just so you know!"

"How come?"

"How you going to almost embarrass the shit out of me in my store to take me out by bus?" I said pointing in the convenience store's direction.

The bus driver then asked, "Are you guys coming in?"

"No Larry, we cool! Thanks!" responded Richard. The bus' doors then closed. As the bus drove, he said to me, "We ain't taking the bus to go where we supposed to go."

"Taxi?"

"Nope!"

"Then how?" I asked, sounding very annoyed.

Richard pointed at the ground. I looked at the ground confused. I asked, "What the fuck you pointing at the ground for?"

He just smiled. I became annoyed and shouted, "*Pendejo!* You better tell me how we going there!"

"We walking!"

I paused and looked at him, just hoping that he'll come up with a *Gotcha* type of smile or expression and then call a cab or have a friend come along with some kind of vehicle, but I was sorely disappointed. So I took a deep breath and said to him, "Before, I verbally minimize you in both Spanish and English, I want you to tell me why you decided to ask me out when you have no means of transport. You have 1 minute!"

"Don't you wanna feel the wind blow while you walking? That's one of my favorite things to do. Just be out here, me and Chicago! I mean, people like nature and all, but the police sirens, the asphalt, all that is nature for me and I wanted to share that with you."

I looked at him and couldn't believe it. He shared the same passion I had. But I was more surprised at myself saying, "Let's go then."

Richard smiled and we started walking. I put my hands in my pockets and walked right beside him. The whole time, Richard was saying things to try to make me laugh. Like a novice comedian, he said a few things which were funny, but also said other things which did not make much sense.

After a good 7-8 minutes' walk, we arrived at a Soul Food joint called Nenette's World. There, the atmosphere was jovial. Two yellow brick pillars, matching the walls, stood at the east and west of little place. About eleven tables were in the establishment; one in the middle and the other 5 surrounding. The place was dressed in African art from wooden sculptures to paintings, which I found very beautiful.

Richard did know a few people in the establishment, which was noticeable, since he was greeted by a few as we made our way inside.

We sat at the middle table. As we waited, I said, "That's a nice place."

Richard said, "Yeah. I like it here. It's a change of scenery."

I took a look at the menu. This place was much more different from the *Artisan de Saveur*. The menus were in English for one and I knew exactly what was being cooked. Not everything needed to be an adventure.

When I knew what I wanted, I put down my menu and looked up only to face the Ghetto King staring at me. I waited for a bit, but it didn't look like his look was going to change, so I just asked, "What?"

"You mentioned having had a bad breakup. What happened?"

The question took me off guard. I was supposed to conduct the investigation. He didn't need to know about me. I looked away and said, "We ain't going to talk about that tonight."

Richard said, "Damn! He must've hurt you real bad!"

I looked at him almost ready to blurt out the pain I went through with Simon, but held my tongue and asked, "How you figure?"

"You're too damn guarded!"

"If I told you anything about it, you wouldn't understand half the shit I went through with that nigga! He put me through hell!"

Richard said, "Ok! You wanna hear about me?"

"Yeah let's do that! What happened yesterday?"

"What do you mean?"

I leaned forward and with a tone just above a whisper and started, "What happened with them cops yesterday? Are they part of a drug smuggling ring and you're their contact with their supplier, but now your group decided to go to war with them?"

At first he looked at me with an inquisitive look. Then he burst out laughing. I felt a little weird. Was it the way I said it? What was so funny?

"You watch too much TV, that's your problem."

He continued laughing. I smiled. I couldn't see what else I could say, considering he was laughing at me. He then said, catching his breath, "Probably cause you're a female and you've yet to experience this, but cops don't really care about people of our complexion. They were fucking with me, so I talked back. They didn't like it, so they took me in to teach me a lesson."

"That other cop was black though."

"So?"

"It looked more intense than that."

"It was . . . Cops just like to fuck with you even when you do legit work."

"Which brings me to my next question . . . What do you do?"

"I do work everywhere around town and I keep enough money to pay rent and eat."

"Which explains you not having a car."

Richard nodded. Realizing his situation, I asked, worried, "Did you expect me to pay for dinner too?"

Richard laughed and said, "You're my guest. You don't pay a thing tonight or every other night that you're with me."

I smiled. This guy is totally the opposite of Simon's flamboyant and money throwing ways. He was cocky, but yet, he was still a gentleman. But this was a onetime thing. There would be no repeat.

I said, "I totally sympathize with you. I can't go down like that though. I don't feel like I'm ready to go with anyone just yet."

He said, nodding, "Oh yes . . . The breakup."

I nodded as well. He then asked, "When did you guys break up?"

Reminiscing on the bad experience, I answered, slowly, "Almost 4 years now."

Richard's eyes widened looking at me. The look surprised me. He asked, "Are you kidding me?"

"What do you mean?"

"Yo, Renee . . . Check it out honey! You gots to let that go! I mean it's been 4 years!"

I wanted to tell him that I was raped and that I had a child resulting from it as well, but he had not gained the right to know about my personal life.

"The way things went down is complicated. I can't really tell you about it."

Richard said, "It don't matter. He can cheat with a million girls, that don't mean you got to let him have power over you like that still! You need to take your life back girl!"

He was right and I did take control of my life. That was why I didn't trust anyone that came my way. That was why no one had access to my heart but my daughter. That was why this was going to be a onetime date.

"Richard, you wouldn't understand."

"Oh I understand just fine! You just a punk! You can't deal with this like a normal human being, so you punking out!"

Punk? How dare he insult me without knowing the facts? Before I knew it, I was up, shouting, "You can't understand cause that motherfucker raped me! Now tell me who's the fuckin punk!"

If I cared, I would've seen that the entire establishment was looking in our direction. He wanted to get some date from me and started insulting me, but he didn't have to live with the memories or the nightmares. But I did. At that very moment, as I was standing, the flashbacks of that animal on top of me were vivid. Like waterfalls, my tear ducts released a warm flow across my cheeks. To me, that meant that it was time to leave this place and so I did.

I started crying uncontrollably once I reached outside. Why did that have to be brought back to my memory? I had been able to go through days without seeing those horrific images. It was only in my sleep that I had to battle them.

I fell to my knees and just cried in front of the establishment, my face in my hands. I just wanted to be held . . . And my wish was granted. In his arms, Richard held me, apologizing. But as tight as he was holding me, all I was feeling was the sweet touch of the wind.

CHAPTER 16

The Start Of A Beautiful . . .

Like clockwork, there he was waiting to walk me to my bus stop, wait for the bus with me and ride the bus with me until I reached my stop.

It never was that easy though. I mean, it took a while for me to be ok with these different aspects of our relationship.

I only saw us as strangers who happened to share an evening at first, but Richard wanted to be so much more though. Since that first day we met, he wanted to be more than just friends and me, I refused to trust that easily.

It bugged me that he saw me cry like that at the Soul Food joint. He came the next day just to check up on me. I thought it was nice and figured that it would end there, but he would not let it.

First, he wanted to walk me to the bus and I agreed, but I told him that I didn't need for him to wait with me. Then, we started talking. That always seemed to be the defining factor that changed things in relationship. We went from being strangers to acquaintances. He gave jokes and he gave me quotes from poets and philosophers. I liked that. So eventually, I didn't chase him away from the bus stop; just chased him off the bus, especially when I knew that he lived in the Southside of the city.

One night though, there we were, at the bus stop, discussing the validity of the phrase *I Love You* uttered while drunk. The conversation was more fun than it was educational.

"I tell you that people seem to be more truthful while drunk."

"Richard, you're probably drunk now."

We laughed some more. Then a police cruiser stopped right in front of us with two officers as its occupants. We couldn't see what they looked like because they had their flashlights in our faces. The glare temporary blinded us. Then, the passenger door opened and a black officer came out. The same one who had confronted Richard on my birthday. He turned off his flashlight and walked towards us saying, "King Richard, what's really good?"

I looked at Richard and he was in a stance I never seen him in before. Actually . . . I did see him stand like that once. It was that first day, before we met, when he confronted them outside the store.

The officer glanced at me and then looked at Richard again and said, "That's a fine bitch you got there. Too good for you if you ask me."

Tightening my fists, I prepared myself. I wanted to beat that officer senseless. I wanted him to eat his words. I didn't want him to get to call me a bitch that freely. But then, as I thought about it, I realized that it would mean jail or even worse, death. I said, "I don't see your mother here, *officer*."

The man looked at me, angry. He stepped in my direction and Richard found himself in front of him. The other cop, a white guy, came out of the driver side and stood next to the opened door, one hand to his side, asking, "Is there a problem, partner?"

The black cop looked over his shoulder and shouted, "Let me check."

He then looked Richard in the eyes and asked, "Is there a problem, dip shit?"

Richard backed away putting his hands in the air, but the whole time, he made sure he stayed in front of me, like a shield. The cop stayed there for a minute and then walked back to his car. We kept quiet Richard and I. We just watched as the car drove away. My fists were still tightened, allowing me to remember why I hated cops so much.

Then I felt the wind, calming me down, the sweet breeze making me release the anger in me. That anger you feel when you can't do nothing about a situation, but you wish you could. That cop pushing Richard around and then trying to do the same with me. I knew now that Richard was not lying when he told me that they kept harassing him. I knew about police brutality and them over stepping their boundaries. More at that time than ever.

That's how it came that Richard travelled with me on the bus, making sure that he was safe with me and away from the police. That's how I came to care for him, although I never wanted for things to be like this. And as we spent more time together, the more and more my feelings for him started to grow. I wanted to keep him safe.

CHAPTER 17

Happyness

Richard was coming to take me to a movie and this little girl was going to get me late. I wouldn't mind, but it was the going to be opening night for this Will Smith flick, *Pursuit of Happyness*. Usually being late meant nothing to me, but on opening night, if we got there late, that meant we got the front seats and we would have to break our necks for two hours.

I checked and saw that it was 4:04 pm on the store's clock. She was late and so was Richard. We were going to miss the 5 o'clock show.

The employee I waited for finally arrived, almost fifteen minutes late; a little freckled face teenager, who started begging me for forgiveness as she arrived, almost as if she was going to go to the electric chair.

I gave her instructions on what to remember prior to closing the store and then, made my way outside.

As I stepped out, the biggest surprise was there waiting for me. A black Chrysler 300 was outside the store and next to it was, the Shark.

Simon had returned and stood there waiting with his signature smile still on his face. He walked towards me and said, "How you been?"

The gaze he kept on me reminded me of the many times we got hot for each other and made out like teenagers in heat. Looking at me with this wanting, this desire. I felt differently. My look showed disgust.

I was not fazed by the surprise appearance by the Shark. For long, I wondered what would happen the day that he tried to come back into my life. When I had those thoughts, I allowed my imagination to peruse through a great selection of violent images, but not that day. I responded, nonchalantly, "Me and your daughter are good. You remember the child you gave me after raping me of course, right?"

Simon's smile disappeared to make place for a serious look. He said, "I'm sorry about that. I had to go out on business, but I recognize the error of my ways. And I am prepared to make it right."

I chuckled and said, "You want to make it right after 6 years? You must've dropped on some serious loot there, dude!"

Simon laughed and said, "Wow! I didn't remember you to be that Ghetto, Renee."

Offended, I pushed him and said, "Let me show you how ghetto I can really be!"

That made Simon move back a few steps. I could see the fear and surprised look on his face. Being the proud man he was, he decided to step forward to me. I didn't back down though. As a matter of fact, I dropped my bag on the ground and put up my fists. Simon took a step back and looked at my fighting stance.

He then smiled and said, "Let's not get violent."

I return the smile and picked up my bag saying, "You're still a bitch!"

You could see on Simon's face that my comment was not appreciated, but I was right. Simon's backbone was as strong as his willingness to be without money, which meant, nonexistent. He then took an envelope from his pocket and gave it to me.

"What the hell is that?"

"Look inside."

I opened the envelope and a large check was inside. I asked, "And what is this?"

"It's part of the money I owe in child support."

"Nice. Your daughter will be very happy to know that."

In the distance, Richard could be seen walking up the street in our direction. That brought a smile to my face and made me ignore Simon altogether. He probably was talking, but my attention was on Richard. As he reached us, I said to him, putting my arms around him, "Late again, homie!"

Richard smiled and hugged me saying, "Whatever."

My pleasant moment was then disturbed as I heard Simon say, "Renee, aren't you going to introduce the father of your child to your friend here?"

I looked at him, annoyed. I didn't want to introduce them. Unfortunately, Richard was a man who enjoyed getting into conversation with others. So he started, sounding excited, "That's Shannon's daddy?"

Simon stepped up and extended his hand towards Richard, and said, "Simon 'The Shark' Smith."

With a smile as big as Simon's, Richard shook his hand and said, "King Richard."

"Royalty!" said Simon smiling at me. He asked, "Are you and Renee an item?"

Richard winked at me and said, "Yeah we are! I don't know what you did to her, but I had to reach here every day with flowers, poems and all kinds of stuff to make this happen."

I smiled and held Richard's arm. I then said, "It would be nice to be here and continue this conversation between the King & the mindless, but we have a movie to catch."

Simon smiled at me and I could tell that my insult was well received. He then looked at Richard and asked, "Is your car down the street, your majesty?"

I looked at Simon with an annoyed look again and said, "Simon, stop it!"

Richard put his hand on my shoulder and said, "No, it's ok. I don't mind."

He then looked at Simon and stepped up to him. I looked at them both and saw that Richard was slightly taller than Simon.

Seeing them stand like this, I could see the contrast that these two had created. You had one claiming royalty by name, he was not full of money, but the manner in which he conducted himself made him deserving of that name. The other was the vilest of human beings, flaunting money probably because he would feel inferior if he didn't do so.

Richard looked Simon in the eyes and said, "I don't mind taking the bus, only cause I get to meet tons of people. I get to meet people as wonderful as Renee and I get to meet unfit parents as well. Anyways, I don't need materialistic things like cars to be happy. I have my health, my girl and your daughter. Right now, that's enough to make me happy."

We heard the limousine door open and close. A strong looking character came out. It was not Eugene. It was just a mean looking dark skinned man in a suit. Richard looked at him, smiled and backed away with his hands in the air, like he did with the cop.

I said, "We really gotta go Simon. It was not a pleasure."

And so we walked away from Simon. I made sure to take one last look back and saw that he just stood there still leering at me like he had done so many times.

In the beginning of my relationship with Richard, I always wondered what would be the outcome of a confrontation between the Shark & the King. I always saw Simon being defeated if things were to get violent with Richard, but in a battle of wits I thought that Simon would be better equipped than the performance he gave against Richard. Instead, Richard showed himself to be the better man, the better man in everything.

The way he handled himself made me proud, but it made me desire him more. I didn't even care that we missed the 5 o'clock movie and had to wait for the next one.

The next day, I was at work again looking through the store's mail wondering why I had to go through the same routine all the time when all that came was bills. It's not like someone was going to send me $10,000,000 tax free, though that would make my day right there.

Just as I was about to give up on looking through the bill collection, I saw a letter addressed to me. No return address was on the letter, just an envelope with the name ***Renee*** written on it. I opened it and started reading,

Your physical beauty seduced my nature!
Your inner beauty changed my plans for the future!
I wanted a woman who could take on what the world will throw at her
I can honestly say that you are stronger than the hardest of liquors!
You make a man who speaks in sign language go speechless
Only because every move you make spells S.E.X.Y.N.E.S.S.
I started my pursuit of you like Will Smith pursued Happyness!
Making my moves strongly and smartly, just like a game of chess!
I really just wanted to tell you that you were out of sight!
Before I forget . . . Join the King for dinner tonight!

I smiled remembering the day before. I remembered the movie, the confrontation and then remembering my entire relationship with Richard; how persistent he was after my breaking down at the soul food joint. I really was not going to give him a chance. He was not the type of guy that I desired, but for an entire year, he came to the store all the time with literature, poems that he wrote and jokes to woo me. He went from a dirty guy who walked in my store serenading me to a dear friend who made sure I healed to this incredible guy I was falling for. Over the course of time, I didn't have any more nightmares. Simon was out of my system.

And when I thought of Simon, I can't get the image of how Richard handled him the day before out of my head. Since Cooper, I never had a guy come to my rescue like Richard had.

Since Cooper, it has not happened . . . I realized that I had fallen in love with Richard. I was really in love with him. I was thinking of him all the time.

The whole day, I was just bubbly all over the store. Seventh Heaven was easy to attain compared to where I was. I was not as annoyed about being there as I usually would. Customers seemed easier to handle.

And just when I thought my level of happiness could not get any higher the end of my shift came and there was Richard. As I stepped out of the store, and saw him stand there with a smile on his face, I couldn't control myself. I just ran towards him and jumped in his arms. Richard, happy, but shocked, attempted to talk, "What . . ."

But I was not having it. I had to kiss him. I wanted to taste his mouth without the complication of words, but he kept trying to talk. Overjoyed, I said, "*Bésame*[25]!"

I then kissed him passionately some more. The kiss was sloppy, but passionate nonetheless. Richard pulled away from me saying, "Ok! Chill for one minute!"

I was breathing heavily, just standing there, smiling, as though I was a lioness in front of a defenseless prey that had nowhere to flee.

Wiping the side of his mouth with his thumb, Richard continued, "Not that I mind all that, but what was that for?"

"Your poem!"

Richard smiled and asked, "So you're having dinner with me?"

---

[25] Kiss me

I kissed him again. Pulling away again, Richard said, "Ok, I'll take that as a yes."

I laughed.

Richard asked, "What did you say in Spanish earlier?"

"*Bésame?*"

"Yeah! What does that mean?"

"Kiss me."

Richard smiled and kissed me in a less sloppy way. He said, "Let's go to my place and eat."

We made our way there, to Richard's place. Through our train ride from Logan Square to Englewood, I was on Richard like a little school girl, just clinging to his arm, hugging him and kissing him, which was different from my usual sitting next to him and telling jokes. From the blue line, we connected to the green line and finished our trip at the Halsted Station, which was a few blocks away from Richard's apartment on West 63rd Street at the Bethel Terrace.

You could see the change of scenery from Logan Square to this place. It was like going in another country. Then again, I've never been to another country, let alone another town. Come to think of it, I've never been outside of Chicago. The building was not in the best of neighborhoods, in the South side of Chicago. A place where police dared reaching very seldom due to the severity of crime sprees, but that didn't faze me. I was in such a great mood, nothing could bring me down or scare me.

As we walked in, we didn't take two steps before we stumbled unto what was the living room/dining area. A round table was set with unlit candles in the middle of it with two chairs facing one another and two empty plates and two empty wine glasses. Next to it was a couch that looked like it had gone through all the major wars in history. A TV set from the 80s was there as well. The kitchen was an open concept which looked like it should've been closed. It was located on the left side of the apartment. Right behind the apartment door, the stove was there looking like it was having a losing battle with rust. Richard went through some trouble to get the place cleaned and it showed. The sink was without dirty dishes. The fridge looked like one of those brown old school 1970 fridges. Parts of his floor felt sticky as you walked. They were old tiles that were supposed to be cream, but more of the brown persuasion. To the right, there was a hallway that couldn't have been longer than two to three yards longer. I saw three doors there and immediately assumed that there was a bathroom, a closet and the bedroom. I knew where I wanted to head to.

I had been on a high which I could not explain. Simon never made me feel that way. I loved my daughter, but that type of high was totally different.

As Richard started talking, I interrupted saying, "How about you give me the tour of your place?"

Richard looked around, confused. He then said, "But that's pretty much it. There's the bedroom, but not much to see there."

"I still want to see it and the bathroom too."

My sudden interest in Richard's small modest apartment seemed to puzzle him. I knew what it was that I desired. I wanted to skip dinner and go straight for dessert.

So he walked towards the bedroom holding my hand. As we entered, he picked up the clothing on the ground and dropped them in a basket nearby. He then looked around the room some more. While he did that, I closed the door behind us. The sound of the door closing caught his attention and so he looked at me.

I then went to the window and closed the blinds, only having sparkles of lights going through them. My heart beating louder than ever, I was pretty sure that he could hear it, but I was walking towards him regardless. I started kissing him again, not in a sloppy way like earlier, but with the same passion. I then pushed him down on the bed and started to slowly undress.

I always expressed to Richard how uncomfortable I was with the whole physical thing, so I was not surprised when he stayed there, in front of me, not moving.

As I stood in my bra and panties in front of him, Richard again, opened his mouth to say something. I interrupted him again saying, "Say nothing. Don't spoil this moment."

Richard complied, with just a look of amazement on his face. I stood there not so sure as to what my next move should be. He sat on the bed waiting on me, but I myself was just improvising.

I then saw Richard licking his lips, and I just allowed myself to act freely and do what felt right. So I kneeled down and began to work on his pants, by removing his belt and then sliding them down. I kept his boxers on, afraid of the harden content which was trapped inside. I looked Richard in his eye and said, "Take off your top."

Richard removed his jacket and shirt, finding himself in a white beater. His tattoos were just showing all over his arms, all over his chest. I was not a big fan of the tattoos on a man, but at that time, I needed Richard. I desired Richard more than anything in the world. And so I got off my knees and straddled Richard, kissing him again.

For a good 15 minutes, we were just in a lip wrestling contest, only because that was the only part of this whole intimacy experience that I was not afraid of, but I knew that I started this whole thing and that I had to end it. Therefore, I removed my panties. Once those were off, I pinned the King on the bed and just stayed there on top of him as though I was a champion who had just conquered my foe. But in this situation, the foe was going to get a prize.

Again, I did what I felt was right. And what was right seemed rough and animalistic. I put my hand on the white beater he was wearing. The piece of cloth was tight on him, but it was on him, not off. Without warning, I ripped the shirt apart and off of Richard's body.

A look of surprise was on the King's face while a look of satisfaction was on my face. His muscular body was filled with more graffiti. I then took a deep breath and as I exhaled, I proceeded to remove my bra and found myself completely nude in front of Richard. That was not the prize though. It was just part of it, an appetizer, some would say. I then stood up and looked at him. He was lying there, looking at me. After taking another deep breath, I removed Richard's boxers and found myself in front of his risen nature.

But I was not there to observe. I wanted to experience. And so, once again, I straddled The King inserting the harden part inside of me, slowly. Every inch of it going inside, made me gasp with a feeling of pleasure.

While I bit my lower lip, Richard held on to my waist. As he was completely inside of me, I stayed like that, taking it all in; the feeling; Richard; the moment. And then, I started moving my pelvis, slowly, not wanting to make any wrong movement, enjoying the slow grind, remembering the first time I did that; remembering Cooper.

I closed my eyes and started to pick up speed as my excitement was just rising with every thrust and motions. With every movement, I could hear myself saying, "*Dios Mio!*"

I didn't know if I was whispering, shouting or just saying it at a normal volume.

I was pretty much in charge, until I felt Richard's arm around me. I opened my eyes and there he was, sitting now, his face close to mine. We kissed as we allowed the room to fill up with an aroma of lust and passion.

Out of the blue, he stood up on the bed, with me on him. Almost automatically, I had my legs wrapped around his waist. My body and desires were in sync with him. This feeling could not end.

We looked each other in the eye. Such an intense moment. I was no longer grinding on him, nor was he trying to thrust inside me. For what could've seemed like an eternity, we stayed like that, touching each other with our breaths. Finally, we went back to the bed, this time, him on top of me.

I whispered, "*Deseo que Este momento pueda durar para siempre*[26]*!*"

Richard looked at me confused.

"*Por favor, hace me el amor*[27]*!*"

Richard still didn't understand. I just kissed him, which brought him back on track. And so he started to thrust and was not going fast, but with more power, which was hurting me a little, but I didn't want him to stop.

"*¡Más! ¡Dame más!*[28]"

It seemed like Richard understood what I requested because he went faster. At the same time, I was providing hip movements making sure I got more from him.

Then the climax came. Though unlikely in any type of sexual encounters, this one climax came at the same time for the both us as I felt him unloading filling me with his juices. Like a chorus from a song we both knew only too well, a loud moaning sound was heard from both of us, which brought Richard to collapse on top of me as breathless as I was.

We stayed there, breathing, feeling each other's chest; each other's heart. Not as intense as my first, but close. A smile appeared on my face, happy I had done that.

---

[26] I wish this moment could last forever

[27] Please make love to me

[28] More! Give me more!

The passion was left in the air, all over Richard's bedroom. We held each other, naked as we were and just as we were going to allow ourselves to go to sleep, I said, "Richard?"

"Yes, baby?"

I looked at him and wanted to tell him that I had fallen in love with him. I wanted to see his reaction. Hear him say, *Baby I've been waiting for you to say that for so long.* Then, I wondered . . . What if he didn't feel the same way? What if he was not that into me? I couldn't risk getting hurt again.

"Baby?"

He was still looking at me, waiting to hear what I had to say.

"Thank you. This was great."

He kissed me with a smile on his face. He then said, "We aim to please."

We kissed again and then went to sleep.

As allowed myself to fall victim to slumber, I tried to capture images of what had just transpired, trying to feel again what was just felt with every movement that came to mind, but then other images came through. There was that animal again, that beast moving violently on top of me. I tried to push those images away. I tried to get back to me and Richard . . . Me and Cooper. But the evil images were taking control. It was becoming too much.

I woke up, screaming, but my screams were cut short as I felt a strong hand around my throat, shortly after I opened my eyes. It was dark in the room. The sun's light was not trying to go through the shades anymore. The night had taken over and Richard was chocking me to death. I felt him squeeze on my neck. I tried to struggle out of his hold, but he was too strong. I looked at him, trying to see what was wrong. I saw an unfamiliar darkness behind his eyes; a darkness darker than the night. I heard him say through his teeth, "Why the fuck are you screaming for?"

I tried to speak, I tried to explain, but his hold on my neck would not allow me to speak. With the little ounce of strength I had, my hands went to his face and I touched it, as gently as I could. I cried because I still loved that man.

He released his hold and the darkness that was in his eyes was gone. I coughed and wheezed, trying to catch my breath. I thought about what was going to happen next. Was I going to kick his ass? Was I going to r0un out like I did that night with Simon? Was he going to finish the job he had started?

In the midst of my planning, Richard started crying. He started begging for my forgiveness. He explained to me how fear made him act a certain way. He told me that he was never going to lay a hand on me again. The screams just scared him that much.

My hands to my throat, I looked at him and I could see the truth in his eyes. I could see his sincerity. I could tell he was remorseful or maybe I loved him so much that I wanted to believe him. It's not like I was a battered woman. I was not the kind of woman who would get beaten up by her boyfriend. I could defend myself if it came down to it. I forgave him . . .

Every time it happened.

CHAPTER 18

The Promise

We laid there on Cooper's bed, under his covers. My head was on his chest, listening to his heart going back to a normal pace, considering we had just finished making love all while the radio belted Whitney Houston's *I will always love you* and other great romantic hits from that year

With my fingers, I traced the lines that formed his 8 packs.

He kissed my forehead and that made me smile.

He whispered in my ear, "I love you."

That gave me goose bumps. It was not a bad thing. It was a great feeling, but why me? I asked him.

With his right hand, he held my face and looked into my eyes for a moment. I held my breath as that moment alone felt as intense as me having an orgasm. He started, "Renee, do you remember the first time I met you?"

I nodded.

"Well, I remember everything before that. I remember the first time I saw you at the beginning of the school year. I saw you keeping to yourself, not talking to anyone. Maria was the only person you seemed to know."

"I can't explain why I love you, but I do. When I wake up in the morning, I can't wait to say hi to you. When you have to go home to your mother's house, I do my best to keep you out longer. When I see you smile, I start smiling."

Automatically, I smiled and he did the same.

"Why do you always ask me that question?"

I looked down and shrugged. He said, "The first time I asked you out, you first told me that you thought I was gay."

I looked at him and said in a winey tone, "The way you talked made me think that you were."

He smiled and continued, "Then when I walked away, you came and asked me, *Why me?* You said that Jessica and Maria were hotter looking girls than you."

I looked down again and said, "Well, they are."

"I know."

I slapped his stomach. He laughed. He then said, "You're perfect for me Renee."

I smiled and said, "You know, I told you how intense things are at home with my mother, right?"

He nodded.

I told him how my mother made sure that there was a line dividing me and Maria, letting us know that we were less than sisters. I told him how Maria was very absent, but when she found out that I could fight, she had me around for confrontations of any kind.

"I love you Cooper, but I need to be sure that you'll never ever leave me. I'm so vulnerable when it comes to you. I wouldn't survive if you left."

He touched my ear lobe softly and caressed my face as well. He then kissed me. While in our embrace, he positioned himself on top of me, caressing my body and then, parted my legs and slowly entered me, without unlocking our lips once. The sensation of it all was so intense, I'm sure he felt my nails on his back. Cooper suddenly stopped moving and looked in my eyes with that passionate look again. He then said, "Renee . . . Not even death will keep me away from you."

CHAPTER 19

Charges

"I want Shannon to come stay with me."

I looked at Simon's beady eyes, wondering what kind of crack he had been smoking.

"So you reach here with some money and you think that you have the right to take *my* child from me?"

"Renee, I think that it would be easier for you. I mean, she comes to live with me and you come visit her. It won't cost you as much to take care of her."

Just a week after that wonderful night with Richard and a couple of days before Shannon's birthday, this asshole had to come to me with that bullshit.

We argued like that for about 30 minutes. Customers came in and we were still going at it. He was trying to show me his side of the story, telling me that it would be beneficial if Shannon lived with him, told me that it would be less stressful on my mother or me, that it would give him a chance to reconnect with his daughter, but mainly staying on the money subject. Telling me that I wouldn't have to worry about spending my money on her and that I could even go back to school and get out of this convenience store. That was the way he wanted to lure me into saying yes.

I was not giving up on my baby. After that half hour of constant bickering between myself and Jaws, I started, "Get out of here, Simon! I have to work here. This is not the time or the place."

"Renee, just consider it. I mean . . ."

My cell phone then rang. I was so happy it did. I ignored Simon and started, "Hello?"

"This is a collect call from the Chicago Correctional Facility from . . ."

Richard's voice came through, announcing his name.

"Do you accept the charges?"

Fear and panic took hold of my heart once I heard his voice. I forgot to answer. It was just too surreal. I was scared. I thought of that night that the cops came after us. I thought of what possibly could've been done. I wondered if they had beaten him.

"Do you accept the charges?"

CHAPTER 20

Lawyer Up

"Mr. White will now be seeing you."

I walked into the small law office. I couldn't help, but look at the young man. I found him quite handsome with his glasses. A black man, but as light skin as Shemar Moore, yet he still looked like he could give Taye Diggs a run for his money and help Angela Bassett get her groove back again. He actually reminded me a lot of Michael Ealy. Except that he didn't have his color eyes.

I was also taken by how young he was and practicing law. He must've been a couple years older than me. I figured his youth was the reason why he was cheaper than most law offices. He probably needed to have as many cases under his name to make himself respected in the law circuit. He asked me to sit down.

As I closed the door behind me and did as he asked, I said, "I'm Renee Rodriguez."

He smiled at me. I found myself blushing right there and then. He had the most incredible smile I had ever seen. He answered, "How about you tell me what brings you here?"

"Right," I responded looking down, hoping he hadn't seen me blush. I then took a deep breath, looked up and said, "Well, about 6 years ago, I got pregnant from this disgusting vile piece of . . ."

"Whoa there!" said the lawyers with one hand up. He then said, "You have to understand that this is not Jerry Springer or Maury Povich. You have to remain professional at all times. You wanna make a habit of that while in court."

"So what? How do you want me to talk? That's how I feel."

"Trust me. When your enemy insults you, throw a compliment and you'll find yourself winning more. The Bible teaches us that."

"The Bible?"

The young man laughed and said, "Yes. It's a book containing words of wisdom inspired by God. It's a pretty big book. It's pretty good too. You should try it."

"A lawyer that's into God . . . Don't the two contradict theyselves?"

"Wow! You're really forcing the ghetto."

In my eyes, he stopped being cute at that point. I asked, "What you mean?"

He laughed and said, "You don't sound natural. You're forcing it."

I didn't appreciate the remark and was about to let it show verbally, but opted against it realizing that I needed his services. Therefore, I followed his advice and said smiling, "You're quite observant."

The young man smiled and said, "That's impressive. You learn fast. So tell me what happened, again."

"About 6 years ago, I got pregnant from my ex. We were dating but the way I got pregnant was just totally wrong. He had dropped *Rohypnol* in my drink and had his way with me."

"Did you go to the police?"

"The police?" I remembered Richard and I remembered my disgust with them.

"Ok," said Chris smiling and taking notes. I guess my response needed no explanation. He said, looking at his notepad, "Please continue."

"Anyways, Shannon was born and she is the best thing that ever happened to me. Mr. Smith was paying child support for that first year after she was born, but his business was going off the deep end. Then he turned up missing. And for 5 years, I didn't hear from him. Now, he came back about a month ago. He gave me an envelope with a big check inside for missing on his child support payment. Afterwards, he came to me saying that he wanted to have a relationship with her and have her stay with him. I kept saying no. Now he just served me with papers stating that he'll fight me in court for the custody of my child."

Chris took a deep breath and took off his glasses. He then said, "I'm not going to lie to you. It's not going to be easy. I wish you had gone to the police when he dropped the Rohypnol in your drink. He would've gone to jail for rape and you wouldn't have to deal with this. The fact that he was away from the child for the past 5 years can be an advantage for you though."

I said, "You have to help me keep my daughter. I can't lose her and especially not to him. He does not care about her. He just wants to stop paying for her. I'm begging you, please help me keep her."

Chris started picking his papers on the desk and said, "I pity your boyfriend."

I was shocked. How could he say something like that? Not understanding, I asked, "What do you mean?"

The lawyer stuck his papers in his briefcase and then walked next to me saying, "I pity your boyfriend, because if you ever beg him like this, he won't stand a chance. I'll take your case."

Chris extended his hand towards me. Excited, I got up from my seat and jumped in his arms, hugging him. He laughed and said, "You have to go to Church and pray. God has to be OUR lawyer in this case. That is, if we want a fighting chance."

I looked at him smiling and said, "Ok. Thank you for helping us though. I'll give you a call if I have more questions."

Chris answered, "Sure. Also, I need you to fill out this questionnaire."

He dug inside his briefcase and found a document that he handed to me. I glanced over it and a bunch of personal questions were on there. I asked, "What's that about?"

"Well, you gave me a nice synopsis on your life. I need to know the full details so that I may start working on a game plan, especially because the father of your child will have to go after your personal life to make a case for himself."

It made sense. He told me that I could fax the filled out form to him as soon as I was done with it. I said, "Thank you, Mr. White."

"Please, call me Christopher."

He did that smile again. The one that made blush. I smiled, doing my best to hide my teeth. Without adding anything further, I walked away.

I was happy with Christopher assisting me, but found him kind of weird when it came to religion. I was catholic, on my mother's side, but never saw the use of it. I didn't require religion in my life. I felt like he was just one of those Christian recruiters who kept throwing religion in your face nonstop. Unhappy until the rest of the world was on their knees praising Jesus. It didn't matter though. I'd let it go from one ear and out the other. I just had to keep my child.

A week after meeting him, I got a phone call from Christopher.

"Renee, you may have a problem with this case of yours."

"What is it?"

"You have to end things with your boyfriend."

CHAPTER 21

Dethroned

Why? Why did I agree to it, I thought?

Richard was a problem to the case? All because the cops were disturbing him?

I explained to Christopher that Richard was having issues with the cops because they liked to fuck with black people. Hell, I told him about that one time he got arrested on that minor charge two months prior. When I got to the police station, he apparently had been arrested for having a joint.

I told him that it was not enough weed to be considered a crime. Christopher understood, but apparently, he said he had to show me something that would explain what he meant.

We went down to Clarke's Diner on North Lincoln Avenue. We got a booth there and waited. My back was to the door and Christopher faced me. The waitress came in jean shorts and a tank top that advertised the name of the place. She took our drink orders and went on her way, giving us time to think about what we were going to eat. I looked at the brick walls and see if they were going to hear the things that would become the deciding factor in the future of my relationship with Richard. Christopher kept talking, trying to reassure me, but I was too anxious to get this over with to pay attention to him. The waitress came back with our drinks and then took our food order. I had never been to Clarke's before, so I just ordered whatever it is that Chris was ordering which was the Kung Fu Chicken.

We waited for the food and barely talked. The place was filled with patrons, but not too loud. I looked out the window which gave a view of Lincoln Avenue. Cars were just passing by, none stopping. I looked in Christopher's direction, but all he did was take notes. I looked outside for another ten minutes until our food came in. The plates of food smelled so good. I was happy and ready to dig in, until I heard Christopher say, "James, thanks for coming."

I turned around to see who came through the front door. A bad surprise was waiting for me. The black cop that confronted Richard and me before we started going together was the one person we had been waiting for at the diner. It was hard to recognize him at first considering he was wearing grey jeans and a black leather jacket holding a briefcase compared to his uniform and gun. I knew that I was not going to believe anything he said.

Christopher stood up and shook his hand. He introduced me and when the police officer turned around to face me, he recognized me. No smiles, no fears, no shock, just professionalism. He extended his hand towards me, but I refused to acknowledge him. Instead, I took a piece of my chicken and ate it without taking my off of him.

Christopher looked at me and him for a minute, feeling the awkwardness that had just settled in. He then asked, "Am I missing something?"

"We met before," said the officer.

I looked at him with a smile and said, "Yeah, he called me a fine bitch."

"Oh shit, James!"

The officer looked at Christopher who was not impressed with what he just learned. I went back to my food. The officer asked, "Can we just get started?"

Christopher moved, giving enough space for the officer to sit next to him. I ate with my mouth over my plate, but my eyes were on the black officer, known to me as James.

He took out documents from his briefcase showing that Richard had been the subject of a drug investigation from the past three years. The reason why he had yet to be arrested was because the cops were looking to find his supplier.

James, however, had a personal vendetta against Richard. Something about a family member of his that was connected to the whole thing, but I was not listening to that part. The documents were valid. Richard was not the man I thought he was. He had lied to me. And that was why Christopher wanted me to stay away from him.

James said to me, "When I saw you the first time, I thought you were involved in what he did. I am sorry for the way we first met."

He extended his hand again. My food was done at that time and I was just shocked by what I just learned. No longer mad at him, I shook his hand. He said, "I recommend that you stay away from him."

"Me too," responded Christopher.

I just nodded, holding back the tears from my eyes. The hurt and pain I was feeling almost made me numb. I hated what I had just heard. How was I going to handle this?

CHAPTER 22

Fight

I was completely disconnected from my surroundings. I was completely confused with everything. I tried to make sense of what just happened. Richard lying to me; it all seemed like an evil nightmare. I couldn't even pay attention to Donnie McClurkin & Yolanda Adams singing through Christopher's car radio about The Prayer they were offering.

But then, my mind focused on the love of my life once we pulled up at Shannon's school just in time for classes to end. As he parked the grey 2004 Toyota Corolla across the street from the school, among the sea of children moving about, I could see my daughter, waiting with a few friends of hers in front of the gates, talking, without a care in the world. Meanwhile, I was fighting to keep her with me. She was oblivious to the craziness this world was offering. I stepped out of the car and shouted, "Shannon, baby!"

Shannon looked around, recognizing my voice, but searching for me. I shouted again, "I'm here, sweetheart!"

Shannon then saw in which direction the sound came from. My baby said bye to her friends and started running towards me. As she was about to reach the sidewalk, a man stood in her way.

The man looked down at her and to my surprise Shannon hugged him. Then I heard her shout in joy, "Richard!"

I just heard the name and ran from the car towards my child, not paying attention to oncoming traffic, but lucky enough that the motorists had good breaks. As I reached there, they were separating from their embrace, but as I saw Richard, I couldn't hold myself. I gave of myself to him, I gave him my heart. Without thinking, I pushed him down. As he fell and connected to the ground, I picked up Shannon in my arms and started walking.

Surprised and on the asphalt, Richard asked, "What's wrong with you?"

I screamed out, as I walked back towards Christopher's car, "Stay away from me and my child!"

The road was free of traffic and so I crossed. As we arrived at the car, I opened the door for Shannon and looked back at Richard as he stood there, looking in our direction. Shannon asked, "Mama, what's wrong? Why did you push Richard?"

I didn't answer. I just sat her in the backseat of the car, secured her with the seatbelt and then went back to the passenger seat I was occupying.

The ride home was quiet. Christopher didn't ask anything and Shannon just sat in the back, looking as sad as ever. I could not even begin to think about how she could feel seeing the only male figure that I allowed in her life to be pushed away like I did Richard. But I was moving on instincts. He was threatening my relationship with my daughter. I could lose her if he stayed around. I would not allow for it to happen.

When we arrived home, Christopher said, "I'll come and get you tomorrow and we'll review the game plan."

I nodded. He then turned to Shannon and said, "Hey you! You probably don't know me. My name is Chris."

Shannon looked at him without saying a word. I looked at her and she looked at me at that time. Then she looked back at Chris and asked, "Are you taking Richard's place?"

I started, "Shannon! Nobody is taking Richard's place. Richard was just not right for us."

Shannon asked, surprised, "How come?"

She wouldn't understand if I tried to explain it to her. I didn't even tell her about her father trying to take her away from me. I just said, opening my car door, "Let's go inside! Say bye to Chris, baby!"

Christopher said, "Bye Shannon!"

Shannon whispered, "Bye," right before I took her out of the car.

I was not happy that Shannon had to see that, but I was less happy with Richard.

Once we walked inside the house, I told Shannon to remove her school stuff and get ready for supper. I then went upstairs to my room and sat down on my bed. I rubbed my temples, trying to let the day sink in. I decided that I would call Chris . . . Just because I needed someone to talk to. As I picked up the phone, I heard, *"Mama, yo no pienso que Renée perderá Shannon.*[29] *"*

"Espere María. ¿Quién recogió el teléfono?[30] *"*

I hung up quick. Why in more than five years, would I stumble on a conversation between Maria and mama and today of all days? I had to go for a shower and clear my mind.

An hour after being inside the house, the doorbell was heard. Mama's heavy footsteps heading towards the front door resonated all the way to my room and after a little while, I heard her scream out, "*¡Dolores, alguien está en la puerta para usted!*[31]"

I walked to the hallway and stood there, at the bottom of the stairs as I saw Richard. My mother was putting her coat on and said, "*Voy a la tienda.*[32]"

"*Bueno, mama.*"

Mama then stepped out. Richard seemed very uncomfortable as he asked, "Why did you push me back there?"

I didn't answer. I just looked at him, with my arms crossed. He walked slowly towards me and asked, "What's the problem, baby?"

I answered, "The truth is the problem."

"What do you mean?"

"You lied to me."

"When did I lie to you, Renee?"

I explained to him what I had to go through; the documents, the officer telling me about his real life, how hurt I was and how upset that had made me. I told him the potential danger that could've had on my custody issue with Shannon.

Richard looked down, ashamed. I was angry at this show of weakness from him. I was disgusted, so disgusted that I walked up to him and slapped him in the face. Richard still looked down. I was about to hit him

---

[29] Mama, I don't think Renee is going to lose Shannon.

[30] Hold on Maria, Who picked up the phone?

[31] Dolores, someone's at the door for you

[32] I'm going to the store.

again, but he held my hand and said, "The first slap was free because I deserved it. The next one will get you hurt."

I looked at him. I was not convinced by this wannabe macho crap, especially after experiencing it with Simon. So I clenched my free hand into a fist and swung at him . . . and connected. Unlike Simon, Richard was still on his feet and unlike Simon; Richard made a sound which was quite unusual. I heard this growling sound from him. And then, out of nowhere, I was laid out by a backhand from him. I was on the ground, just hurting. His strength was much greater than anyone that ever struck me before.

Richard kneeled down next to me and put his hand on my face, almost as to caress it, saying, "I didn't mean to hurt you, baby, but you pushed me to it."

At this time, I didn't want to hear anything. I looked at him and saw tears in his eyes. More weakness. It pissed me off. I yelled out, "You're nothing but a pussy!"

Richard got up and took a couple steps back still looking at me. I got up as well, with a little difficulty, with one hand on my cheek. To my own surprise though, I threw another punch, but with more power. Before I could acknowledge the pain in my knuckles from connecting with his jaw line, he was holding me by my shirt collar and flinging me across the hallway.

The pain in my knuckles was history at this time. I was on the ground, holding my head which had connected with the wall. I looked up and saw Richard standing as the pitiful King that he was and then, very much unexpectedly, he kicked me in my side. The kick was not light. Richard was looking to inflict major damage on me. I didn't know what was harder to do, get over the pain or breathing.

I was on the ground holding my sides and wheezing. I saw blood coming out of my mouth. That probably was internal bleeding. I then heard a voice behind me, a voice that brought fear to my very soul.

"LEAVE MY MOMMY ALONE!"

Shannon had seen the scene and came to my aid, in her own way. She stayed there, crying and Richard walked towards her. I got up as best as I could and stumbled towards Richard. I had to keep him away from her. So I still tried to make my way to him, I started saying, "You . . . You're nuh . . . You're nothing, buh . . . A coward! I'd rather . . . fight . . . A bitch!"

As I reached close enough to him, Richard put his hand on my throat and shouted, as he squeezed, "You are a bitch! I never tried to hurt you, but you pushed me today!"

As I started gasping for air, feeling my life slowly fleeting away, I felt his tears come down on my face as he said, "I'm sorry!"

He was going to kill me. He wanted to kill me. I looked at his face as I did so many times and saw the darkness in his eyes. I recognized that darkness. Before, I thought it was there by mistake. At that time, before my untimely death, I knew it was meant to be there. Richard's true self was coming out.

It was not my time to go though. I was not going to die. The air flow started to be normal again. The squeeze on my neck was released and I was dropped to the ground. As I fell down, coughing and gasping, I saw Richard moving on the ground almost as though he was having a seizure. I looked up and saw Chris standing over my defeated attacker.

In his hand, he had a taser gun, which seemed to have been the weapon that rendered Richard powerless. Chris went to me as I was on the ground still gasping for air. He kneeled down next to me and asked, "Are you ok?"

Trying to speak, I asked, "How . . . ?"

Chris said, as he looked me over, "I was driving away and I saw him walking over to the house, and something told me nothing good could come out of this, so I drove back and waited. When I called your phone, no one picked up. I waited 10 minutes, then I charged in here and miraculously, the door was left opened."

He then dialed on his phone and started, "Hello, police. I'm calling to report a domestic violence situation. The victim is a woman in her late 20s and possibly a child under the age of 10. I took out the aggressor with my taser. I also need an ambulance for the woman because she's been injured. My name is Christopher White and we are located at 1420-A Kostner Avenue."

Richard stayed there, at my side, unconscious. Shannon was on my other side, hugging up on me. I could feel her shaking. The child must have been terrified by what just happened.

Never had I thought that I could get beat the way that I did, not since I learned how to fight. I thought that I could at least hold my own against a guy like Richard . . . The man I was supposed to be in love with . . .

CHAPTER 23

Court Is In Session

When I woke up that morning, I thought that I was going to enter the same courtroom Jack Nicholson entered and uttered the famous phrase *You can't handle the truth!*

I expected a Judge Judy lookalike to be there, because she hated men like Simon. I expected a jury of my peers who would see the evil inside the man who was trying to steal my main reason for living.

I thought that everyone would see my battle wounds inflicted by my ex boyfriend. A man I had fallen in love with and whom I thought had fallen in love with me as well, but was able to lay hands on me.

Instead, Simon and I were going to do battle inside a boardroom. The boardroom had glass walls and giant windows along with a double glass door.

Chris and I were the first ones of the two parties to arrive and we met the mediator who was already sitting at the head of the table, in his two piece grey suit, blue tie and white shirt.

The table was long enough to sit 20 people and the room was big enough to hold two times that number. The smell in it was different than all the other places. It smelled new.

The mediator was going to play the role of judge and jury. Chris recommended that I whisper in his ear whenever I needed something, but if I wanted to be out loud, not to let my emotions take the best of me. I wondered if I would be able to be professional with him. I had become comfortable enough to call my lawyer Chris instead of Christopher. All the times we went over the game plan, he reminded me to call him Chris. So it finally settled in my head.

The mediator did not want to engage in small talk, even after we tried. He only gave short answers. He would not bite, so we kept quiet like he did.

We didn't have to wait more than 10 minutes before Simon and his lawyer walked in. His lawyer looked like Mr. Drummond from Different Strokes. I sat there looking at the man, hoping my stare would be so intense that he did get a stroke. Then again, my stare was not that intense. It was more inquisitive.

The mediator, after shuffling around some paper, started, "Before we start, are you expecting anyone else?"

Chris looked at me and I shook my head no. We immediately looked in Simon's camp and nothing. The mediator, put down the papers and said, "All right, let's get . . . uhm . . . started here."

Simon's lawyer started to talk about Simon's situation. He made it sound really good. Better than what I remembered. Made his hiatus sound like a much needed reality check. He didn't speak on my relationship with Richard. I was done with Richard. His majesty was in jail. My feelings for him had changed, but a part of me still loved him. It was hard to believe that six months before this court date, he almost took my life.

Chris then spoke about me and he mentioned that I was the only parent Shannon had known and that Simon was given the opportunity to be a part of her life, but walked away on his responsibility.

And then, as soon as Chris was done speaking, here came the kicker; the one thing that shocked each and every one of us, except for Simon and his lawyer. Simon's lawyer said, "In regards to Shannon, my client does not wish to take full custody."

CHAPTER 24

Losing Shannon

"Mama, do I really have to go?"

My poor child. She was still innocent, still oblivious to the wiles of this world. I quickly dismissed her question and told her how beautiful she looked, dressed in a red and white polka dot top and a black knee length skirt, her hair in ponytails.

That's what I thought I would do, until we got to the front door like we did six years ago, when I found Maria in there. But this was different.

Unlike last time, we rang the doorbell and he let us into the building.

As we arrived at his apartment door and knocked, Shannon was not eager to enter, like she did so many years ago. I was not looking to get inside either. I wanted to retreat and walk away. But I had to do it. We agreed.

She had to be with her father and as we had agreed in the proceedings with the mediator, Shannon was to spend every second weekend at Simon's place.

For an entire month, he came over to the house and met with me and Shannon. We wanted for her to be familiarized with him considering that she didn't remember him. Every weekend, he would come and say hi and spend 2 hours with her. On his visits, he would sometimes bring gifts for Shannon, just to get her to like him more. A little of what he did when me and him dated.

But then, I regretted my decision I made when we were with the mediator; when Chris whispered in my ear that we should take the deal that Simon's lawyer made.

That's how I felt when I saw Jessica opening the door; the same Jessica who attempted to make my life miserable in high school; the same Jessica whom I had the opportunity to beat up in Simon's office. She opened the door, with a look that said she was victorious. That she had won. I took Shannon's arm and put her behind me.

Still smiling, Jessica said, "Well . . . Well . . . Well . . . Small world, isn't it?"

My breathing intensified. I was ready for battle, as though her wolfpack was about to jump me again. I asked, "Why are you here?"

She was about to answer, but I interrupted and said, "Besides, the obvious."

She chuckled and then said, waving the back of her left hand in the air like a lighter at a concert, "I'm the woman of the house. Soon to be Mrs. Smith."

An expensive ring rested on that finger giving truth to her claim. I felt the anxiety rise within me. Jessica being engaged to Simon meant that Shannon was in danger.

She then looked at my precious child and kneeled down, her face still dressed with her smile.

"Are you Shannon?"

I looked at Shannon as she responded, "Yes."

Jessica extended her hand to greet her and just before Shannon could do the same, I pulled her back behind me and asked, "Where's Simon?"

Jessica stood back up chuckling. She went back inside the apartment, door still opened.

Shannon asked me, "Mama, what's wrong?"

"Wait a minute, baby."

I saw Simon walking down the hall making his way to us. He asked, as he reached the door, "Why didn't you walk in?"

"Simon, why didn't you tell me that Jessica was living here with you?"

"Why does it matter?"

"You know the history between me and her. You probably know also that she is going to hurt my child to get revenge on me."

"You're paranoid, Renee. We've all grown up. You should try it as well. This whole rivalry with Jessica is done. She's done with it."

"You're an idiot if you believe that. And if she does try to do something to my daughter, you'll be in charge of her funeral instead of a wedding."

"Again, stop acting crazy."

"Whatever Simon! Why is she here?"

He admitted that he started seeing her while we were together, just a few weeks after the beating I gave her. She apparently went chasing after him. He also revealed that she stayed by his side even after he lost his money. He had fallen in love with her and when his fortune was returned to him, he proposed to her.

After explaining himself, he squatted so he could be at eye level with the reason why I was present. Shannon smiled at him as he extended his arms for an embrace. I didn't want to let go of her. I was in defensive mode and I wanted to remain on the safe side.

Simon held on to Shannon's hand, which she had extended towards him and looked at me with a look that said, it's ok. I released my hold on her and Simon picked her up in his arms. He asked, "How are you doing, sweetie?"

She softly said, "Fine."

Through his visits and our visits to his place, she had grown accustomed to him, but not enough to call him daddy. He tried to get her to do it, but Simon had to understand that he had made it difficult for that to happen easily, considering he left for so long.

They were interacting, that I was sure of, but I didn't care at that point and time. I was distracted by the fireman axe which was covered by glass next to the extinguisher with thoughts of Jessica.

I got a few calls from time to time by Christopher, every weekend that Shannon was spending at Simon's place. I didn't tell him about Jessica. I should've, but I didn't want to. I didn't see the point in boring him with the whole issue from my childhood. I didn't want to have to talk about my past life.

The third month that I had to bring Shannon over, Jessica greeted us at the door again. I had told Simon that I didn't want to see her when I dropped off Shannon, and he made sure of it that second time, but it looked he forgot about it. I was very unhappy, but then surprised when I saw Shannon just jump in her arms, saying, "Hi Jessica!"

Jessica hugged her and said, "Hey, you little brat. Go inside! I got a surprise for you."

Shannon ran in and I shouted, "Hey, aren't you going to say bye to me?"

She stopped dead in her tracks and ran back to me. She hugged me goodbye and left in the direction of her new found treasures. I watched as she disappeared inside the apartment and when I couldn't see her anymore. I decided to make my way out of there.

"Your daughter is a beautiful child. She must get that from Simon."

I stopped walking and started allowing all kinds of replies to flow through my head without allowing my mouth to speak them out. I took a deep breath and as I exhaled, I continued walking.

"You're really a stupid bitch, mulatto."

I made a U-Turn and walked back towards her. I was going to give her my undivided attention. That was what she wanted from me. As a matter of fact, I was sure that she wanted for me to give her a beating. I didn't want to disappoint.

I stood in front of her, towered over her actually. She was looking up at me, like she did so many times. We were going to battle again. It was inevitable. A light push was the only thing that was needed.

"If you knew what was good for you, you'd be in this house instead of me, with your child. Instead, you lost this great guy. I guess the only people you can keep around are fools like that faggot boy! His faggot ass . . ."

She was talking about Cooper. I knew that. A light push was the only thing that was needed, but she broke down the walls of my common sense and sanity. The rage that subdued my being was uncontrollable at that time. My statement to the police would read that, along with the history me and Jessica had. The police would ask me about the scratches on the right side of my face and I would tell them that the bitch was able to get her hands on me. I would tell them that I punched her in the face repeatedly. They would correlate that information with the hospital medical records showing that a few teeth were missing from her mouth. I would describe how I stomped on her repeatedly as well. That explained the broken ribs to the cops; apparently, she had a similar injury in the past.

Simon's side of the story was different than mine apparently. He would explain how he got home and restrained me from stomping on his unconscious fiancée all while Shannon was looking.

"Rodriguez, you've made bail!"

It was very late at night. I had made the only phone call allowed to me to the only person whom I thought could and would help me out about a few hours after my fingerprints, pictures and statement had been taken. I stayed in jail for a few more hours and was relieved when I heard the guard.

I felt shame as soon as I sat down inside Chris' car. That was a nervous habit of mine. I knew I had done wrong and I expected to get scolded. I didn't even look in his direction. I just looked down in shame as I buckled my seatbelt.

He didn't start the car. He didn't ask any questions. Silence was in charge, but it could not be for long. I started, "I'm so sorry, Chris. I'll pay you back, I swear."

Chris let out a long and loud sigh.

"Renee . . . Do you know what your actions have caused tonight?"

I refused to answer. I stayed quiet. I was too ashamed to respond. It was as if I was speaking with my mother. Not talking, hoping that the scolding would go faster.

"Renee, you've lost Shannon. Simon is going to go for full custody and win."

CHAPTER 25

Her Best Interest

"Doctor Holstrom will see you now."

We were lead through the mahogany doors and into the doctor's office.

He was sitting behind his mahogany desk, finishing up notes on some papers when we walked in. Without looking up, he said, "Take a seat."

All three of us sat down. I just wanted to get this over with. I needed to get back to a normal life and this man probably had the solution for it.

We waited a little while before Dr. Holstrom put down that pen and said, "All right. I apologize, my last patient was very complex."

He then looked at us with a smile and said, "So, from what I gathered on the phone with your wife, Mr. Smith . . ."

I interrupted him saying, "I'm not his wife. He's the father of my child, but we're not married."

He nodded in acknowledgement and said, "I'm sorry. From what I gathered, there seems to be an issue with Shannon. She is afraid to be around you, Ms . . ."

He started to look on his clipboard and then said, unsure, "Rodriguez?"

I looked at my little girl who was sitting away from me, while Simon was in between the two of us. She was still afraid to look at me. When came time for her to come back to the house, she would not be alone in the same room with me. Instead, she'd be with my mother at all times. She didn't want to go to Simon's house with me, but she would go ahead and wait in her room, alone waiting for him to come pick her up.

I was convinced Doctor Holstrom would be able to find a solution to my problem.

"Well, I'm going to need for the two of you to step out at this time while I speak with Shannon alone."

I looked at Simon and he didn't seem to disagree, so we stood up and left.

We sat in the lobby, listening to the secretary's typing and phone answering techniques. We sat opposite ends of a brown leather couch. The lobby was filled with those inspiring photographs with the words COURAGE or PERSEVERANCE and the little quotes at the bottom.

Simon was looking through his palm pilot, typing a few things. I was just looking at the mahogany doors. I was waiting for her to come out of there, wanting to jump in my arms. The image of that thought in my head put me in a relaxed state. I just needed for it to happen.

"Renee?"

I jerked out of my happy thought and was faced with an unpleasant reality. Simon was trying to do small talk.

"I said you looked good."

I looked at my blue lace pencil skirt and my black and blue layered color block top. I looked at him with a look that said that I was weirded out. I said an unimpressed, "Thanks."

He flashed his usual smile. A smile that I once found cute, but now, I hated and despised. I looked away to prevent myself from throwing up.

During our wait time, I caught Simon leering in my direction more than once. Same cocky look he had the first time we met at the club. At that time, it was intriguing and attractive. Now, I was too suspicious of him. As far as I was concerned, anything he did was with an ulterior motive. As a matter of fact, I was sure that he was responsible for the situation that I was in.

Then the mahogany doors opened again. There, Shannon came out. I had high hopes. She came out smiling. My happy thoughts were going to come true, but reality was a cruel bitch. She went to Simon. I looked at them and the doctor said, "Miss, could I please see you?"

I looked at them for a little bit, envious and hurt. I had to understand what was going on. I walked in hastily and sat on the chair in front of his desk. Before he could say anything, I asked, "What happened?"

"Miss, your daughter suffers from Post-Traumatic Stress."

"How did she get that?"

"Shannon has described in details two different situations where she witnessed violence. The first time was with this Richard character. She said she saw him kicking you over and over and her being powerless and crying. She also remembered you pushing him down at her school. That altogether confused her. The second occurrence was when you were kicking this Jessica character whom I believe is involved with Mr. Smith. You refused to pay attention to Shannon when she begged you to stop. She heard you utter the words over and over, *I'm going to kill you bitch*."

My heart was in my throat as I remembered every event the doctor mentioned. I was not sorry for doing what I had done in my past. But I started regretting them when the doctor said, "I believe it's in Shannon's best interest to stay with her father."

CHAPTER 26

Sacrifices

"Why did you ask me here Simon?" I asked standing in the hallway of his apartment.

The proceedings for Shannon's custody were underway and things were not going so good. A restriction order had been placed against me. I was not allowed within a hundred of Jessica and she was there with my child, but it was more than just that. My child was terrified of me. I tried to get her on the phone, but she refused to talk to me. I never stopped calling to speak with her, even though she didn't respond. But I found it weird that Simon asked me over almost three weeks after our visit to the psychiatrist. It was a text message but I probably should've called before going. It would've avoided this.

He stood there, at the door, alcohol on his breath, in a wife beater and jeans, with a bottle of grey goose in hand; a look that was beyond cliché. He said, looking at me with hunger, "You're looking good, did you know that?"

I looked at myself, my white coat on, my blue jeans and my black boots and then I looked at him. Sounding exhausted, I asked, "Is Shannon here?"

He took a sip of vodka and said, "Nah, she stepped out with Jessica."

"Where?"

"England."

I licked my lips, annoyed and asked, "What.Do.You.Want?"

He smiled, not his regular smile where all his teeth were showing as if he were in a Dentyne commercial. The smile he had was cunning. He was up to no good. His thoughts were impure.

He placed one hand on my belt and I slapped it away. He got angry and said, "Do you want to have Shannon back?"

I started breathing loudly. I was scared of what he was going to request. I was ready to do anything to get my child and I meant, ANYTHING. I asked, "What do you want?"

He placed his hand on my belt buckle again. I started shaking as fear took hold of me.

Simon said, "You know what? I always regretted spending only *one* night with you . . ."

He then looked at me in my eyes and I could recognize the lust in his as he pulled me towards him. He said, "I think it'd be nice if we got it on one more time!"

I remembered when I beat his ass in this same hallway so many years ago. I wished I could do it one more time and ridicule him again.

I looked at him, angry, tears running down my face, fearing what I knew I had to do to get Shannon back.

I asked, "Will I get Shannon back if . . ."

I couldn't say it. I cried, just thinking about it. I was physically sick. I wanted to throw up. Simon said, "If you don't do it, it will be much more harder for you to get her back."

"How?"

He chuckled and said, "Let's face it. What she really needs is to be back in the house with you for a little while and things will be back to normal."

I always knew that. I knew it. But now, for that to happen, I had to do something that would add further scars to my subconscious, but was necessary.

I closed my eyes and asked, "Can I use your bathroom first?"

Simon licked my neck and then whispered in my ear, "Sure. I'll be in my room, wearing my favorite suit."

"What suit you talking about?"

Simon kissed my lips and said, "My birthday suit."

Simon then winked at me and walked away, laughing at his pathetic little comment he made, happy of what just transpired. I cried as he walked away.

I took a deep breath, trying to gather myself. I then made my way inside the apartment and inside his bathroom.

As I closed the bathroom door, flashbacks of my nightmare came back, the beast of a man standing over me, like a wolf slobbering over its catch, but in this case, a shark. I had made sure to forget about those images and as the years went by, I had become pretty good at it. But that night, I knew that I was going to get the sequel to that nightmare. I looked at myself in that mirror and watched the bags under my eyes from all the crying over the years. Those bags were getting heavy and it looked like I was going to add on more.

As I stood in front of Simon's room door, I had knots in my stomach. I tried to make things easier for myself by thinking of worst things I had done in life, but soon realized that this was beating every single evil deed I ever committed.

I probably stood in front of that door for a good ten minutes. Everything in me said, don't do it, but my heart alone ached for my child. The reasoning in my brain said that Simon was not one to be trusted, my heart said that I had to do everything required to get Shannon back.

Finally, I put my hand on the knob. My hand was shaking uncontrollably as I allowed myself to cry. Because of my hand shaking, I had difficulty to get a good grip on the knob and thus, couldn't get the door opened that easily.

Finally the door opened, but Simon was the one who had opened it, with a smile on his face. He said, "Get in."

I walked in slowly, wiping the tears from my eyes and then, I heard the door close behind me, with a click. I looked back and saw that he had locked it with a key. Simon put the key in his pocket and pulled out a condom. He then pulled down his pants and boxers.

He was obviously ready. His large erected girth stood there looking at me and I looked at it disgusted. I wanted to get it over with, so I took off my clothes and lied down on the bed. Simon asked, after putting on the contraceptive, "No foreplay?"

I answered, "Let's just get it over with."

Simon smiled and said, "I love it when you talk like that."

I was feeling more sickened hearing his comment. I laid there on my back and closed my eyes, waiting. Simon, unromantically, moved himself on top of me and violently, made his way inside me. Being dry, I let out a scream from the pain. I guessed that Simon felt the dryness as he stopped everything and went to his drawer. He picked up a bottle of lubricant and made his way back to me. He applied some on my vagina and said, smiling, "Looks like some things never change with you."

I was angered by the remark and wanted to attack him for saying that, but instead stayed on the bed, frustrated, reminding myself that I had to do that if I wanted to get my daughter back.

Simon went back to the drawer and returned the lube. He then said, trying to sound sexy, "Now, let's get it on."

Maybe my disdain for Simon made it so bad for me that I felt sick to my stomach. Regardless, Simon went back in again. The lube had made things easier for him to go inside of me, but I still felt pain and was letting it known with the little painful moans I couldn't hide at every thrust given by the Shark. I closed my eyes again, trying to imagine something less offensive. However, my eyes closed brought me back to those flashbacks I had been having. The flashbacks became clearer. I was able to make up the face of that beast on top of me. The same face belonged to the shark that was currently having his way with me.

Though it only lasted about a couple of minutes, I felt like it was too long. As he reached his climaxing plateau, the man moaned so loud, it sounded like a moose getting tortured in some forest. I could feel drops of sweats falling from his forehead onto my face.

Simon then seemed to have come to end of his race as his breathing intensifies and then made the most awkward and stupid looking face before collapsing on top of me, out of breath and sweaty. Unfortunately, it wasn't over. I tried to get up and Simon proceeded to put his hand on my right breast and attempted to massage it. He was hurting me more than he was pleasuring me. He then started sucking on the other breast. He looked at me and I just looked back at him, wondering what he was trying to attempt. He kept on going looking at me, maybe hoping to see some type of signs that I was enjoying myself, like biting my lip or a moan, but all he got was a look that said, *what do you think you're doing?*

Upset, Simon pushed me off the bed and said, "You're better in bed when you're drugged up. You got more rhythm!"

I got up from the floor angry and yelled out, "*Pendejo!*"

I then said, as I was putting my clothes back on, "I don't need this shit from your dumbass! I'm just going to get the fuck up outta here! Just make sure to bring my daughter back when she's back here."

"You get her when I tell you!" said Simon still lying down, not even looking in my direction.

My heart sunk in my chest, held down by fear. I knew this could happen, but I was wishing that there he would actually help me get Shannon back. While fear still held on to my heart, I asked, "What?"

"You heard me. Now get the fuck out of my place!"

"Simon, I want my child!" I said crying, "You said I could have her back."

Simon looked at me and said, "I told you, you'll get her when I tell you!"

"After this shit, you're going to renege on your word?"

"Renege? I didn't know you knew big words like that Renee. Have you been reading?" asked Simon, smiling.

I threw my shoe at him. Simon ducked just in time. He then threw it back at me, but instead of ducking, I deflected it with my arm. It was hurting me, but I didn't want to show it to him. He didn't need to see anymore signs of weakness from me.

I allowed tears though. Allowing was not even the proper word for it. My body was betraying my every command. I surrendered to this mutiny and put my head down in shame as they strongly flowed down my cheeks. Simon obviously not fazed by it, said, "Stop that bitch ass crying and leave my place. Oh and by the way, don't call me. I'll call you!"

His words resonated inside my head the entire time I walked home. I wanted to go to bed and sleep and forget what happened just, hoping that Simon, regardless of his drunken state, could show that he had a heart and give me back my child. Then again, that would not happen.

When I arrived, my mother was at the door, dressed in a flowery dress and her hair down. The smell coming from the kitchen told me that she had put in work, obviously expecting some good news. She saw the look of disappointment in my face, along with the brown paper bag. She asked, "*Donde esta Shannon?*[33]"

I took off my coat and said, "England."

"*Nunca viene atrás?*[34]"

I took off my boots and responded, "I don't know."

---

33 Where is Shannon

34 Is she ever coming back?

"*Eres una chica estúpida. No merecen a ese niño maravilloso. Eso fue llevada lejos.*[35]"

I refused to listen to more and just started to walk upstairs. My mother kept talking and attacking me while I walked away, my brown paper bag in hand. I reached my bedroom and closed the door behind me and in her face. I could still hear her talk for a little while and then, she walked away. I waited, wanting to be sure that she was gone and after five minutes, that was confirmed. So I placed a pillow, a sheet of paper and pen on the floor. I took out the bottle of Patron and the razor blades from the brown paper bag.

I laid myself down on the floor and looked at the paper and pen and then the razor blades. I needed encouragement. So I started drinking.

---

[35] You're a stupid girl. You didn't deserve such a wonderful child, that's why she was taken away from you.

CHAPTER 27

My Help Cometh . . .

My cell phone started ringing around 10 am, waking me up. I woke up with a paper next to me and a blade. Although I was still asleep, hung-over and very tired; I remembered what almost went down the night before. Everything I was feeling, I added to that paper. Everyone that I could remember . . . Maria, Shannon, mama, Richard, Simon, Christopher, Cooper . . . My father . . . I decided to forget about how close I was to ending it all and try to make it through the day.

Every movement made me want to vomit especially as I tried to turn my head, looking for my phone that kept ringing. With my hands, I felt around me to see where it could be, like a blind woman. I refused to open my eyes. I wanted to get back to sleep, but to do so would require for me to find the phone. I would stop looking for it every time it went to voicemail, but the ringing would start again. My hands were not up to the task, so I opened my eyes and got up, but found it as I got up off the floor. I had slept on it. I answered and it was Chris on the phone, saying, "Hey, what are you doing today?"

I answered sounding bleary, "Sleeping!"

I then hung up and dropped on the pillow trying to go back to sleep. The phone rang again, and after a few rings, I became very annoyed. I picked up, shouting, "WHAT?!?"

Chris on the other end, said, "Come to church with me."

"No!"

I then hung up again.

The phone rang again. The more it rang, the more I became irritated. Still sounding groggy, I answered, "Are you going to leave me alone if I go?"

"I'm downstairs, so, you better start getting ready!"

I started mumbling some curse words under my breath. Christopher asked, "Excuse me?"

"*¡Usted es un dolor en mi culo!*[36] I'm going to get ready!"

Christopher laughed and I just hung up. I then went to the bathroom to take my shower, but ended up throwing up first. I went to my purse and picked up a bottle of aspirin. I swallowed a couple of pills and then took my shower, in disbelief that I agreed to go to Church with that man. I had never set foot in a Church before, except when I got my confirmation as a child, but that was not the problem. What was I going to wear?

Dressed in a bath towel, I looked at my wardrobe. I remembered that when I had that problem, I'd call Shannon to come in the room and assist me, but that would not happen. My best looking clothes had some revealing aspects to them. I only had one outfit that looked good and proper. Looking at that outfit, I felt like calling Christopher and telling him that I changed my mind. I took another look at it and then made my decision.

Thirty minutes later, I stepped out, a can of Red Bull in one hand, a Spanish Bible in the other and sunglasses on my face, wearing the business suit that Simon bought for me the first and only Christmas we had spent together. Christopher was there as he had said earlier. He was lucky enough to see me walk in that grey business outfit; with that hair style inspired by the ladies at LYD, except that it was in a ponytail.

I didn't feel beautiful though. I was feeling a throbbing headache which was disguised by my moodiness. I figured that as long as I was mean and moody to everyone, they wouldn't ask me questions about my business. But being away from my daughter hurt me, more than anyone could imagine. All of that was weighing on my mind, along with the headache caused by the heavy drinking I had been doing.

As I stepped inside the car, Christopher said, "You are absolutely breathtaking!"

---

[36] You're a pain in my ass

The darkness of my shades allowed my blank stare to show that I couldn't care less for his compliments. I said, "You going to keep looking at me or you going to drive this thing?"

Chris looked at me first and then asked, "Are you ok?"

"Let's see. You wake me up to go to Church and once I'm in the car with you, you end up talking about how I'm taking your breath away. Are you going to break into songs and start singing *The Greatest Love Of All*?"

Christopher closed his eyes and started whispering some sort of prayer under his breath. He then took a deep breath and said, "You're right. Let's get going to Church."

Before taking a sip of my Red Bull, I whispered, "*Mocoso*[37]."

I was pretty sure that Christopher had realized at that point that inner beauty was truly different from outer beauty.

As we arrived at *The Assembly of the Living God Church*, also known as the ALGC, the spirit of the place could be felt from the parking lot. We barely set foot inside the place, and we were greeted with songs of praise to the almighty.

It appeared as though we were late as we walked in the midst of the song service. The ushers guided us to the front pew for us to sit down. The Church, rectangular in shape seemed like it could sit close to 500 people. The pews were arranged in two columns. There were three entrances; one at the back and one at the right and left side of the Church. We came in through the right side of the building. The choir sat behind the pulpit.

The song which was being sang was quite interesting for me, as it went well with the Church's name,

Don't Try To Tell Me, My God Is Dead
He Woke Me Up This Morning
Don't Try To Tell Me He's Not Alive
He Lives Within My Heart
He Opened Up My Blinded Eyes
And Set Me On My Way
Don't Try To Tell My God is Dead
I just Talked To Him Today!

---

37 Punk

Everyone was standing as the song ended, clapping and praising and shouting, with their hands in the air, "Hallelujah! Amen!"

I took off my sunglasses and whispered in Christopher's ear, "Is it always a party like that when you go to Church?"

Christopher smiled and whispered back, "No! They're usually loud."

I looked at him shocked. He started chuckling and I allowed a smile to kill my scowl. Then the choir started harmonizing. A few people were still standing. And on cue, the entire congregation started,

> *Jesus Is The Answer, For The World Today / Above Him, There Is No Other. Jesus Is The Way.*

I couldn't help but be drawn by the lyrics of the song. Could it be possible, Jesus being the actual answer for all of my problems? A man started a solo,

> *I Know You Got Mountains That You Think You Can Not Climb / I Know Your Skies Are Dark; You Think The Sun Won't Shine / I'm Here To Tell You That The Word Of God Is True / And Everything He's Promised, He Will Do It For You*

I was really taken by that verse. I kind of wished I knew of those promises God had made. I looked at my Bible and wondered a bit.

I always thought that Christianity was about doing good deeds and you'd be rewarded for it, and I tried to live by that as much as possible, but with everything that I had to face in my life, I wondered if it was just fairy tales. I missed Shannon and funny enough, I also missed Maria.

A man in a suit walked up to the podium as happy as ever. He looked like a thick Morgan Freeman. He looked to the congregation and said, sounding like Ving Rhames, "Are you happy to be in the house of the Lord today?"

A few scattered 'Amen!' were heard in the crowd. The man said, in a louder tone, "Now that must not be God's people that was singing so beautifully earlier. Otherwise, they would know that David did say *I rejoiced with those who said to me, 'Let us go to the house of the LORD.'*"

The congregation was louder as they all shouted, in one accord, "Amen!"

The man responded, "Now that sounds more like it!"

He then looked around and saw me. He pointed at me and said, "Young lady, you're new here, aren't you?"

I looked around hoping that he was pointing at someone else. He then said, "You, young lady in the grey outfit."

I smiled and nodded yes. The man asked, "Please stand up for everyone to see you."

I looked at Christopher, who just like the man at the pulpit, was all smiles, which irritated me, because I was put on the spot. Knowing I was in Church, I knew I couldn't let out a few curse words under my breath, but I was thinking them though.

I stood up and then turned to the Church and greeted them with a wave of the hand. As I turned back to look at the man at the pulpit, a young man was standing there, holding a microphone in front of me. The man at the pulpit asked, "What is your name?"

Feeling very awkward, I answered in a very shy tone, "Renee."

"Sister Renee!" said the man, "I'm Brother Trevor Michaels. I'm the shepherd of this modest flock you see here. Today, my young sister, I guarantee you that God will speak to you!"

The young man was still there with the microphone. I looked at him and then looked at Brother Trevor. I then gave a fake smile, but polite nonetheless and said into the microphone, "Ok."

"You can take your seat."

He then turned to the man responsible for my coming to the Church and said, "Brother Chris . . . It's been close to a month since the last time we've seen you. How are things for you?"

The young man with the microphone went and stood in front of Christopher. He, in turn, stood up and said, "I've been good pastor. I was just working hard on getting a friend to come down."

The pastor looked at me and then smiled. He then turned to the congregation and said, "Today, I want to direct this sermon to those who are heavily burdened. Those who feel there is no hope in sight, who think that this is the end of the road. I come to tell you that there is still hope! God is that hope! But how can you be so sure? I tell you the Lord has provided a way. God has made provisions for every single problem you have in life. In the book of Psalm chapter 121 from verses 1 to 3, David says,

> ‘*1 I lift up my eyes to the hills—where does my help come from?*
> *2 My help comes from the LORD, the Maker of heaven and earth.*
> *3 He will not let your foot slip—He who watches over you will not slumber*’

If it is written in this here Bible, then it is truth. The Word of God has provision for all things that we require. It is like money in the bank. You just have to make a withdrawal. The problem is that some people do not believe that they have that type of provision in the bank of God. God said that it was there, but the Devil added this doubt in your mind, which makes it hard for you to take advantage of those promises. I tell you, whether Sister Odelle is hurting for money, or Brother Jackson needs a kidney or . . .”

At this time, the pastor looked around and his eyes were planted on me as he said, “Or even if you lost a child, a sister or a loved one, God has something in His Word for you!”

I was shocked. Why did he look at me like that? How did he know? I looked at Christopher and he looked just as shocked as I was. The pastor continued, “In Greek Mythology, there was Antaeus, the son of Poseidon, God of the sea and of Gaia, goddess of the earth. Antaeus was a gigantic wrestler whose strength was found in the earth. Everytime he was knocked down to the earth, he would be stronger. I say that you can all be like Antaeus. You have been knocked down, but God will make you strong again. I tell you today that it is when you're weak that God is strong. And I tell you also that it is in God that we can find our strength. It is not in mere human efforts that you will surmount these difficulties. Humble yourselves so that God can take control and assist you in this here battle. God is calling you today. Please take with me the book of Matthew 11 verse 28 to 30. Jesus tells us,

> ‘*28 Come to me, all you who are weary and burdened, and I will give you rest.*

> **29** *Take my yoke upon you and learn from me, for I am gentle and humble in heart, and you will find rest for your souls.*
> **30** *For my yoke is easy and my burden is light.'"*

At this time, the pastor was shouting, "I tell you, today is the day! God is calling for you! Surrender your heart to God today! He will comfort you! He is the comforter!"

CHAPTER 28

Payback's A Bitch!

"Amen!"

My mother smiled as Christopher finished praying. I smiled back at her. We had such a better relationship since I accepted the Lord in my life.

We stayed up talking about the end of the world, the mark of the beast, the afterlife and about how to get there. My mother couldn't stay up and went to sleep, leaving us to talk.

After a few more Church encounters, I had become a devout Christian woman. I had given up plenty of things such as secular music, makeup and earrings. I even started filtering what I was watching on TV. If it did not edify me in Jesus Christ, I would not listen to it or watch it.

That first message from Brother Trevor really touched me, as all the other ones I heard going to Church. I started giving the title of Brother and Sister to the people I was talking to at Church. At first, I was very uncomfortable thinking this was the beginning of the David Koresh movie, but then I was better and got used to it.

While the world was celebrating a black president in the White House, this religion thing was giving me a new outlook on life. My situation with Shannon remained painful. In the time passed, Simon was given full custody of my child. At the same time, I was given visitation rights, supervised. I was hurting but I had help. My Bible was the assistance I required. Everything I was learning, I would tell Shannon over the phone or when I saw her, whenever Simon brought her over.

Speaking of Simon, my nightmares and flashbacks completely ended. I was suffering from positive thinking only.

My mother liked this new outlook on life and seemed to have softened up on me as well. She was not as rough with me as she used to and at times, she would still try to apply that tough love she had shown before. I was not affected by that anymore though. I had God and I was content with that alone.

With Christopher, I recognized somewhat of a romantic interest that he could've been having for me. He just never seemed to mention it. I couldn't help but be equally attracted to Chris as well, but I was still not trusting men after being burned twice.

I trusted God only and not man.

I took everything that was said in the Bible literally. I was not going to believe anything else. But I was intrigued by Christopher. I wanted to know what was wrong with him. In Simon, I found the devil incarnate and in Richard, I found a demon in disguise, but in Christopher, what could possibly be there?

We were just sitting in the living room, on the old couch, TV turned off, sipping on juice. Then without thinking, I asked, "Do you think that married couples are still married in Heaven?"

Christopher looked like he was a little taken by surprise with that question. He took his time to answer before he said, "Well, I remember Brother Trevor telling me this one day about marriage. He said that his wife was like his land which was promised to him by God and his children are the fruits of that land. At any time, you have to be ready to protect the land just like the people of Israel had to do after as they fought the philistines and other nations trying to conquer them."

I asked, "So, am I Simon's promised land cause I was fruitful?"

Christopher smiled and said, "Not at all. Simon was a pretender who took the land before the man who was promised for it got there."

I smiled. Christopher continued and said, "Now to answer your question, if God promised you a land, why would He take it away from you when you arrive in Heaven? If you get there before your wife, she will come back and you will be together. If she gets there before you, you will get there and be with her."

"That's an interesting analogy. So your girlfriend is your promised land?"

Christopher chuckled and said, "I don't have a girlfriend."

"Fiancée? Wife? Soon to be someone?"

Christopher laughed and said, "I'm single, Renee. I was seeing this girl, but things were not working out. She kept moving in and out of the city."

"Interesting."

Then an awkward silence settled itself in the room. Both of us did not dare look at each other. Though I didn't have as many romantic encounters as most people did, I was able to recognize that silence. I knew that it only took one look for the both of us to get caught up. But with this new outlook on life, I had sworn to celibacy, so I knew I was not going to allow myself to be weak, though I wanted to. I knew what had to be done. I started straightening my purple and white printed dress. I took a deep breath and said, looking away from Chris, "I think it's time for you to go home."

Christopher, got up and said, "I had a great time tonight, Renee. God bless you and take care of yourself."

He then stepped out. I stayed there, just taking in this whole conversation, not knowing what to feel. I wanted to be indifferent and take it as though it was any other conversation I had before, but I knew better. I saw Tyler Perry's Why Did I Get Married. I found out about the Hero Syndrome and realized that I would not allow myself to be getting feelings for a man because he was helping me out.

The next day, I was working the late shift at the same convenience store I had been working at for so long, the one place that barely changed, along with my house which was also the one place where I thought I was safe.

A few minutes close to closing, I stood behind the counter getting ready to close down the store. Lynda Randle was singing about Beulah Land, a place I would love to reach.

At the counter, I was tallying up the numbers for the night and out of the blue a man wearing a ski mask rushed inside the store, shotgun in hand, shouting, "Get your fucking hands up bitch! Get them up!"

I obeyed. I started praying in my heart, looking for that feeling of reassurance I had when I first accepted God in Church, looking for it desperately, because death was standing in front of me with a 12 gauge shotgun. It was kind of ironic when I actually had written a suicide note with a blade next to me.

The man then looked around the place, still pointing his weapon at me. When he talked, it seemed liked there was something in his mouth.

The longer the man was there, the more I started to believe that God had decided that tonight would be my last night. The man still shouting, asked, "Is there anybody else in here?"

I shook my head no, thinking about my daughter that I wanted to hug one more time; my mother I wanted to hear utter the words I Love You; my sister Maria I wanted to reunite with; Chris, my somewhat love interest I was trying to suppress; my father I never met; Cooper . . . Cooper . . . I missed him so much.

The man scared me out of my thoughts as he shouted, "Give me everything in the register! Make it quick and don't try nothing funny!"

I went to the register, opened it, and emptied it in one of the store's plastic bags, in the clumsiest of ways, due to my entire body shaking. I handed the bag over to the gunman and then stepped back with my hands in the air again. The man looked inside the bag and then after seeing that he was provided with the goods he required, he said to me, "Now, I'm going to leave. You turn around and I'll be out of your life for good."

I turned around as per the man's request, having my back facing him. I then waited to hear the store's door to open and close to turn back around with relief, but the gunman seemed to still be inside. The few seconds he had stayed in without saying a word felt like an eternity, with me having my eyes closed and praying for safekeeping. Then the last thing I heard was a voice which was familiar, saying, "Payback's a bitch, Renee! And so are you!"

CHAPTER 29

The Wind

"From dust to dust . . ."

I remembered as the minister was giving his last rites to Cooper. While his friends and family paid their respects, I sat there, black veil that I stole from mama covering my face. Did they know that I was his girlfriend? No. To them, I was a classmate who had grown close to him. But only if they knew . . .

My heart was breaking as I sat down in that pew, as I watched Cooper's body being taken away without me receiving that last kiss . . . That last embrace . . .

I got my last "I LOVE YOU" from him . . . The night he died.

It was graduation night. A month after Tupac Shakur was gunned down and a few months before the Notorious BIG would share the same fate.

Cooper was coming to get me. He called me before he left. I was supposed to wait by my bedroom window. I would look outside and there he would be, waiting for me. We would run to the bus station and head to another city in another state and just live our new lives there.

Cooper was gone before he could make it to my house. He left Chicago without taking me with him. All it took for him to go was a blade. He was taken from this world . . . From me.

The police report stated that he got in an altercation with a young man. The young man had a knife on him and after having been attacked by Cooper, he lodged the weapon in Cooper's thorax several time. He was arrested and charged for involuntary manslaughter, but because he was defending himself, he was released. After finding out that Cooper knew Muay Thai and Jujitsu, the police said that there was validity to the young man's statement.

To them, it was not possible that Cooper could've been attacked by this guy. It was not possible for them to conceive in their minds that Cooper was defending himself from a man with a knife; even though that man had been named in a mugging in the city previously. This time though, he had robbed me of my love.

My heart felt empty. It was as if I was the one that had been stabbed over and over again.

I cried tears upon tears hoping that the casket was empty and that Cooper would come from behind me and just hold me, tightly, my arms over his, feeling his breath on my ear, but when I arrived at the Church, his lifeless body laid there. He looked different. He was more pale than usual.

They allowed for us to walk up to the casket and take one last look at him. I did more than that. I wrote him a letter that said that I would always love him, even though he broke his promise that even death would not keep us apart.

I thought back on the abortion, the many nights I spent crying regretting that I had killed our baby, wishing I could do it over again and stop myself from doing that just so I could have a piece of him with me.

I missed him so much.

Once at the cemetery, I looked down as they filled his tomb with dirt. Again I wished he was there, holding on to me while his family stayed there, holding on to one another. I was not welcomed in their little circle, although I was more deserving.

As I walked away from Cooper's grave, as I made a few steps towards W. Buena Avenue, about to exit Graceland Cemetery, ready to walk towards Lake Michigan, not knowing what I was going to do when I reached there, I started to feel his presence. I looked around Graceland, searching in the distance, but couldn't see him.

Instead, the wind started blowing. I was not going to notice anything, but when I started to feel the wind between my fingers and under my arms, I started to wonder. Was the wind pushing me or was it holding me? Then I felt it touching my ear and I knew it. The connection was too familiar. I couldn't deny it.

Cooper was keeping his promise.

CHAPTER 30

Darkness

Darkness was there, just surrounding me. The peacefulness was almost serene, yet eerie. The afterlife was not as I thought it would be. No white light or voices calling out to me, just nothingness. I wanted to go ahead and speak to God and ask him *why*? I understood that the first few years of my life, I had not given much thought about Him, but what was the deal with me? Why was I going through all of this?

I then started to feel a sharp pain in my back and also started hearing voices. Death was over and afterlife was starting. I couldn't make up what the voices were saying and I tried to open my eyes, but I still felt pain in my back. The pain again, was too much to bear and therefore, I was in darkness again. Before I completely blacked out, I could make out the voice of Christopher shouting, "Renee!"

Nothingness again. No sign of afterlife or God coming around. I then felt a hand on my face. Maybe, that was God. But then I heard, "Mama!"

I didn't think that The Almighty would call me mama. I felt that I had the strength to lift my pupils. So I opened my eyes and saw Shannon standing next to me with one hand caressing my face. I smiled proudly knowing that even if I was not dead or if I was not in Heaven, having my child with me that way was more than comforting. Seeing her there was as if I had woken up from a nightmare into a dream.

I looked around the room and saw Christopher, my mother and Simon. I looked around and realized that it wasn't my bedroom. It wasn't my house period. I wanted to talk, but the inside of my mouth felt really sticky. I tried to say something, but Christopher started, "Don't talk too much, Renee. You've been out for 4 days."

In a slow, soft speech, I asked, "What happened?"

Christopher answered, "You were robbed and shot at the convenience store. Someone heard the shots and called 911."

I looked at my daughter and still smiling, I whispered, "Hey baby."

I tried to move in her direction, but something was wrong. My legs were asleep, or at least, so I thought. I tried moving them again, but nothing. I found it difficult to breathe, I was so scared. I looked at everyone around me and they seemed to have a look of pity on their face. I tried moving my legs again, but I was still unsuccessful. I looked at Chris and my mother and asked, panicking, "Why can't I move my legs?"

Christopher answered, "The two shots damaged some nerves. It . . ."

Chris looked down. With whatever strength I could summon, I attempted to move my upper body upward, so I could see everyone properly. Even that task seemed hard to accomplish, but not impossible. I shouted, "It what?"

The answer was obvious, but I was hoping to hear something reassuring from their mouths, although everyone's demeanor showed nothing reassuring.

Chris looked in my eyes and said, "It paralyzed you from the waist down."

I could not be paralyzed. I had to be able to get up again. I had to be able to walk. It must've been a dream or a nightmare of some sort. I probably was being tested by God. I was going to walk again. I knew I was. But as I used my brain power to do so, nothing happened.

"How is that possible? How can I not walk?"

Damn it, my legs had to start moving. I didn't care for what people or doctors thought, I had to walk, even I had to force myself to do so. I started punching my legs, screaming, "Start moving! Move, goddamn it! MOVE!!!"

Christopher rushed to me, saying, "Shh! Renee, please calm down."

In the midst of my ranting, I was able to hear Simon shouting, "Hey! We need somebody in here! She's getting out of control!"

My punching was interrupted as a group of nurses and doctors held me down. I screamed and shouted, "NO! Let me go!"

My arms were being held back and I wanted to kick, I tried to kick, but I was unable to do so. I was stuck. I was powerless. I was weak. All I could do was cry and cry as loud as I could. I felt the sting of the needle and continued crying and I continued to do so until I returned to the darkness.

As I lost consciousness, I saw Shannon, in tears, being taken away by Simon while I was taken away from a dream to fall right back into a nightmare.

CHAPTER 31

The Return

I started to get the hang of the whole darkness thing. It was better to be in the darkness than to feel the pain and hurt of reality. I was happy like this.

But the thing with the darkness was that it brought me back to reality at any given moments, not knowing what I would see when I woke up. Most of the times, I woke up and saw my mother asleep on the chair, the night outside, IV attached to my arm, my legs still paralyzed. But I would always go back to sleep, crying.

But the one time I came to during daylight, I thought that I was dreaming.

My dream said, "Hey sis!"

I tried to open my eyes and focus on the mirage that I was facing. I knew that it couldn't be another patient. Simon, in an unlikely show of kindness, paid for a private for me to stay in; then again, the hospital staff thought I was too wild to be sharing rooms with other folks. Once my eyes got to focus, I could not believe who it is that was there. Maria was right there in front of me. I asked, "Is this for real?"

Maria walked up to me and hugged me hard saying, "*¡Es real!*[38]"

I wrapped my arms around her, as tight as I could, not letting go, in case she might disappear again. After a good 5 minutes of hugging, Maria sat back down and asked, "So . . . How have you been?"

---

[38] It's real

The question was met with a blank face. Then, automatically, we both laughed.

I asked Maria, "What have you been up to, all these years?"

"I've been here and there. I actually got me a descent gig about 4 years go. I'm a secretary for this record company. I go by Juanita now."

"Why?"

"Well, I wanted to start new with everything, so I decided to change everything. Use my middle name as my first name and stay away from anything familiar as well."

"I guess that's good."

Maria stood up and went to the window. Avoiding my look, she said, "I heard about Simon taking Shannon. I swear; I fucking hate that guy!"

I wanted to join in the hate talk of Simon, but I decided to show Maria that I had turned a new leaf. So I said, "To hate him would be a waste of time. Trust in God, Maria. He'll give me justice."

Maria looked at me smiling and said, "Mom, told me about you turning into a Church girl."

Again, we both laughed. She sat back down and said, "Renee, I'm . . ."

Tears got in the way of her words. I knew what it was she wanted to say and I knew it hurt her too. I opened up my arms and called for her. Maria came into my arms, like I did the night I ran from Simon's place and just like I did so many years ago, she let out her tears. In a distorted voice, she said, "I'm so sorry for what I did to you! I'm so sorry!"

I just held on to my sister, saying, "It's ok. It's ok *querida*!"

After hugging a couple more minutes, Maria sat down, wiping her tears from her face and in an attempt to lighten the mood, she asked, "So, what is it like to fall out of consciousness?"

CHAPTER 32

Revelations

A week had passed. Maria's job sent her out of town and she would not be back for the next 6 months. I had learned that the shooter that night was Richard. He had come out of jail and just set out to get his revenge on me. He took his life a few hours after the robbery and left his ring next to him with a note asking for the ring to be buried with me, obviously thinking that he had shot me to death. I almost envied him. He had taken the easy way out. He was not going to feel pain again. He was not going to be disappointed again. He was not going to be hurt. Thoughts like that reminded me of the blade and note I left but then, I started thinking about the teachings from Church and tried to find comfort in them.

Sleep had become like those game shows where you had to pick a door and see what stood behind. Except that I was not choosing doors. I was choosing when to wake up. When I did, I'd either be alone or someone would be there visiting, like Christopher or my mother. But then, this one time, I woke up and there sat Mr. Samuels in a chair next to me. I looked around to see if anyone else was there. He said, "Don't worry. I mean you no harm."

I asked him, "The store told you what happened?"

"Well, yeah . . ." answered the old man looking down. He then said, "I came down as soon as I heard."

I smiled and said, "I'm glad I have a dedicated customer like you, Mr. Samuels. It makes me feel appreciated."

The old man continued, with tears running down his old wrinkled face, "I'm just glad you're ok."

It was weird to see him cry like that. His James Earl Jones voice sounded weird too when he was choked up. I thought that he must really be dedicated to start crying. Then again, we were kind of close me and him. I had been working at that store for so many years and he was a regular, always bringing gifts on my birthday. I could understand why he was crying, but I didn't want him to. So I tried to be playful, as we always were in the store and asked, "What's wrong, Mr. Samuels?"

He wiped his tears and said, "There's something that I have to tell you, *mi hija*."

Still smiling, I asked, "What is it?"

He took a deep breath and then started to shake, as though he was afraid to say what was on his mind. I looked at him, perplexed. The man took a deep breath again. He opened his mouth and began to shake. I began to get scared thinking that maybe he was reacting to an existing condition he probably had. I asked picking up my nurse buzzer, worried, "Do you want me to call you a nurse for you?"

He got up and quickly grabbed the buzzer from my hand. He shook his head no, as tears ran down his cheek and sat back. He then took a deep breath again. Finally, he let out, "I'm your father."

My eyes widened. My breathing became louder, as though it was my turn to hyperventilate. I looked down, gasping. All these years I had been looking for my father, he had been right there with me. But it was not possible. It couldn't be true. Mr. Samuels was playing or he was probably saying that he felt like he was. I said, playfully, "Mr. Samuels, you need to stop playing!"

The man said looking in my eyes, "I am not playing. I am your father."

I couldn't help but believe what he was saying as I saw the tears and pain in his eyes. I looked at the same man I had known only since I had been working at the convenience store after finishing high school. My relationship with him was somewhat of a father/daughter relationship, but it didn't make sense to me. The man was looking to reconcile years of neglect through measly appearances at the convenience store where I worked. What happened to all the Christmas' and birthdays that he missed before that? Did he ever think of it? Was a he aware of the hurt I went through with my mother because of him? Then questions I asked myself about my father all my life came back to my mind.

With nothing but fury in my eyes, I looked at the man who claimed to be the father who had left me all this time. I asked, "Why now? Why couldn't you be there all this time? Why now?"

Still tearing up, the old man looked up at the ceiling as though he always knew that question would be coming to him. The old man took a deep breath again and then said, "I tried, I . . . I always tried. I never stopped trying. I always tried to be there, but Conchita would not let me come, especially after what happened to Alejandro."

I moved back looking at him, not understanding. First I tried to understand the names. Who in the hell was Conchita? Then I remembered my mother's middle name was Conchita. Alejandro . . . That was the name for Maria's father. Mr. Samuels wiped his tears with a tissue and then asked, "You don't know what happened?"

I answered, "He was murdered."

Mr. Samuels, intrigued, said, "No, he was not. He killed himself."

I was shocked. Alejandro, Maria's father was not killed, but committed suicide. I was about to ask another question, but then, before I could utter a word, the old man took out a picture and gave it to me. I looked at it and saw 3 people on the picture with a baby; 1 woman and 2 men. I recognized my mother on that picture from pictures I had seen at home in a white flowery dress. I also recognized Maria's father and Maria on the pictures from pictures at home, but the other man was a black man in a police uniform, with his arm around Alejandro, who also was wearing a police uniform. The same man that was on the picture, I recognized him as he was a younger version of the man who sat in the chair next to my hospital bed. I asked, "You knew Maria's father?"

"We were best friends and he was my partner while we were on the force."

I was extremely confused. I didn't know what to think of the whole situation.

"Why haven't you come to see me before I started working at convenience store?"

Mr. Samuels answered, "For the first 3 years of your life, I did my best to come see you, but your mother did everything to keep me away. She was so upset over what happened with Ale. So I kept being around the neighborhood. I was at every graduation you ever had and sometimes I would be around your school taking pictures of you."

In an attempt to lighten the mood, I chuckled and said, "Sounds kind of stalk-ish, don't you think?"

My wannabe father chuckled as well and said, "I guess you could say that."

He then took out an envelope from his pocket and handed it to me. I looked through it and saw pictures of me, some out of focus, but I was able to recognize myself on them; most of them during my childhood. I lightly smiled, seeing myself there, out of the lens used by someone who loved me. I cried a little. I asked, "Tell me everything. From the time you met my mother to the last time you saw me."

Mr. Samuels spoke about how he met mama after Alejandro came back from a trip to the old country where he got married. The first time he met mama, he said that the two were taken by one another the minute they saw each other. But they both loved Alejandro too much to let anything happen. At one point, after Maria's birth, Alejandro had taken leave to go visit his mother who was ill in Puerto Rico and asked Mr. Samuels to go by the house from time to time to make sure things were ok mama and Maria. Well, the first night he went to see her, they were in each other's arms, while Maria was asleep. That went on for the entire time Alejandro was gone. When Alejandro came back, he learned that his wife was pregnant. When he found out who was the father of that baby, he took off and was later found gun in hand, bullet in the head. Mr. Samuels said that mama never forgave herself or him for the death of Alejandro, so she made sure that I never saw him. He tried to be respectful of her wishes, but after a short while, he missed his daughter and moved back.

Everything came into perspective for me. I understood why my life was the way it was. My mother hated me for the death of her husband. For the mistake she made with another man, I had to suffer at her own hands.

While I tried to absorb this little history lesson, my mother walked in. As soon as I saw her, I looked at her angry. My mother looked at me and then at the man sitting next to me. It took her a minute to realize who he was. She then asked, "Leon? Is that you?"

"Yes, Conchita," answered the man, as he stood up.

Mama flared up and shouted, "*¡Usted es hijo de la grande puta!*[39] You have no right to call me by that name! I told you to stay away from Dolores!"

That name, Dolores, was signification of why my life was so fucked up. My mother blamed me for what happened and called me Dolores which meant pain. Not anymore!

"My name is Renee! *¡Mama, él me dijo que todo!*[40] I know why you despise me now! *¡Sé por qué usted me llamó Dolores!*[41] I know why you always tried to hurt me with your words. It was because your husband ran off after learning that you fucked another man!"

Mama, apparently hurt by my comments, said, "*Soy su madre.*[42]"

"*No importa ya.*[43]"

"*Seguramente, usted no lo significa*[44]."

"*¿Significó usted dolerme como usted hice todos esos años?*[45]"

Mama looked around the room. What she looked for, I didn't know but she was looking for it. When she realized she couldn't find it, the old woman ran out crying, probably feeling the pain that I had felt all those years while I was under her roof. It was almost retribution for me. Mr. Samuels was still standing there, looking at me. I started crying with both hands covering my face as I told myself that I should be happy because I got some form of retribution from all the verbal abuse given by *Conchita*, but that was not what I wanted from all of this. I wanted love from my mother. Not to hurt her back.

---

39 You son of a bitch

40 Mama, he told me everything!

41 I know why you called me Dolores!

42 I'm your mother

43 It doesn't matter

44 Surely, you don't mean it.

45 Did you mean to hurt me like you did all these years?

CHAPTER 33

Third Time's The Charm

"I'm in love with you, Renee."

I was shocked. He didn't even warm up to it. He just blurred it out. He continued, "I know you've been hurt in the past. I mean, I can see Simon's ways and how he did hurt you, as well as Richard, but I'm not them. In no ways am I like any of them. I can't give you the lifestyle of glamorous dinners in chic restaurants or shopping at expensive boutiques and I can't send you poetry because my inspiration goes as far as my wallet will at the boutiques."

I laughed. Christopher smiled and said, "I want you to know that I can make you happy though and I guarantee your happiness only because I feel like I'm dying whenever I see you sad."

I smiled as I never received a declaration of love like that one.

"Wow. I . . . I'm speechless."

Christopher walked to my bedside and took my left hand. He then went on one knee and took out a black velvet box from his pocket. I didn't need to hear what would happen next as I seen all kinds of romantic movies in the past depicting that same scene over and over again. I looked at him and asked, "Are you about to ask me to marry you?"

"If you let me place a word in."

"*Dios Mio!* But we didn't even date. We just talked."

Christopher asked, "You mean to tell me that you couldn't see it through our interaction together?" asked Chris looking at me, with eyes that said, *I know you knew.*

I knew that there was something and I liked it because it was safe. But marriage? That was too much. Christopher said, "I prayed about it, I. I know my heart and I know that I love you. I can't help how I feel about you. when I think about the next ten years, I see you by my side."

"Why do you want to marry me though? I don't get it Chris. It makes no sense to me."

Still holding on to my hand, he looked in my eyes and started, "The first day I saw you walk into my office, I thought you were breathtaking. I was attracted. Then when you got shot, I thought I was going to die."

He was still kneeling down and I was taking each and every word in. He continued, "I do not want to lose you, Renee."

I couldn't tell him that I was going to be his wife. I had to think of Shannon and work on that. The situation had not gotten any better. I had met my father for the first time not too long ago and I had just reconciled with my sister Maria.

It was not like I saw him as a boyfriend type, though; I knew that there was an interest there. It was too soon for me to approve of anything. I didn't even know that we were courting, sort of. But I recognize the same kind of interaction I had with Cooper and that reassured me.

"Chris, I can't tell you that I don't have feelings for you cause I'd be lying. But you're going to have to give me that same chance you had to pray about this thing and let me pray on my side. I mean, I want to get to have the opportunity to come to the same decision you came to."

Christopher said getting up, "That's fair enough."

He bit his lower lip as placed the box back in his pocket and then said, "I'll get going now and cancel the *She Said Yes* parade."

I laughed and then said, "Chris, please come here."

Chris walked up to me. I tapped on the side of the bed for him to sit down. As he did so, I held the back of his head, pulled him towards me and planted a kiss on him.

"That's to let you know that I'm really going to pray on this."

Christopher smiled and said, "Well, I'm not going to cancel the parade. I'll just postpone it until further notice."

I laughed again. The young lawyer looked down and then said to me, "You know one thing about you that I'll always love?"

"What's that?"

"Your willingness to fight, regardless of the circumstances, whether it is in the courtroom going against the justice system or in your house against a big dude like Richard. You will fight no matter what. That's why I know you'll beat this paralysis."

I looked down humbled by his comment. I was humbled because I knew that he was wrong.

CHAPTER 34

Sinner

"Amen!"

Pastor Trevor Michaels just finished praying for me. He and his wife came to visit me. He would have come earlier, but he said that he had been on a trip out of town.

I had a burning question though. I wanted to understand why my life was so messed up. Why did I have to go through all of this? Why give me all this misery? Didn't I deserve happiness?

He was looking at me with an awkward smile; making me self-conscious of my situation. He had to say something. His wife shared the same look, but she was not as noticeable as the preacher.

An uncomfortable smile dressed my face. I didn't know what to do or say. Hospital sounds were just filling the room along with the awkwardness.

Finally, he broke the silence and said, "Is there something on your mind, my sister?"

It was my time to formulate my thoughts in a way that I would be understood. I didn't know what to say. So I blurted whatever was in my mind, "Does God hate anyone to a point where He wouldn't allow them to be happy?"

He didn't seem shocked by the question. It was more like he was expecting me to ask that. He started nodding and said, "My dear sister, God does not hate you. You must understand that the rain falls on the just and the unjust, meaning, that anyone will fall victim to good or bad situations."

I smiled politely and said, "Thank you, pastor."

He cleared his throat and said, "There's one thing you have to remember my dear sister."

I looked at him and waited to hear something deep about how God loves me or something along those lines. He continued, "Now is the time to be careful. You do not want to listen to those evil thoughts the Devil will try to subject you to."

I nodded in agreement, but I was not really paying attention until he said, "Before you believe the Devil's lie, you have to deny God's truth and that's when you begin to sin. And you know, as I said it many times in Church, that sin is unbelief in the Word of God."

I nodded again. He stayed and shared more about the Word of God, his wife adding her two cents every once in a while. I appreciated that visit because Pastor Trevor Michaels was a great man. I just knew that after that day, I would not see him again because I decided to give up and become a sinner.

CHAPTER 35

El Extremo Del Dolores

As per usual, the nurses helped me bathe, but that day, I was being discharged. No more hospital gown or hospital food. I was going back to regular clothes and I was going to go home. Three months of it was enough.

The weird thing was that I would have to start living with mama again. We'd have to ignore each other all over again, but this time, it would be more extreme.

A wheelchair was given to me and I started moving around the hospital waiting for Chris to come and pick me up. I wanted to get used to it, so I did circles around the establishment.

The ride home was one that I wanted to forget about. I wanted everything to pass by fast so I didn't have to deal with my mother.

Unfortunately, once we arrived at the house, my mother was there, on the porch sitting down at the top of the little stoop of stairs, looking out, as if she was waiting for someone.

When Chris parked his car in front of the house, I looked at mama from the passenger seat. We locked eyes and had not stopped doing so. A bit of grass separated by a walkway that couldn't be longer than five yards was between us, but it felt like she was already in my space. Still looking, I said, "Let's get it over with."

Chris walked out and went to the trunk. He picked up and unfolded my wheelchair from there. He then rolled it to my side of the car. He opened the door and picked me in his arms. I had not stopped watching my mother. Chris sat me on the chair and I rolled myself towards the house. Chris hurried behind me and as he reached, he put his hands on the wheelchair handles to move me towards the house, but as I felt him pushing, I said, "I don't need help moving towards the house, Chris."

He obliged and walked by my side. As we reached the porch, Esperanza asked, "They let you out?"

I nodded. I asked, "Maria told you?"

Mama shook her head no and said, in a Spanish accent that was still very strong, "I was not expecting you. But I'm glad you're here."

Mama walked down the four steps that led to her porch and sat down on the second step so she could be at height level with me. I looked at Chris and said, "Can you take the stuff in the car and bring them to my room?"

Chris nodded and made his way to the car. I asked mama, "*¿Cómo ha sido usted?*[46]"

She nodded, "*He tenido mejores días. ¿Y usted?*[47]"

"*Mismo.*[48]"

We both looked at the ground at this time and stayed quiet for a moment. Chris walked in on the awkwardness and then asked, "Where's your room?"

Mama answered, "Go upstairs. It's the second door on your right."

Chris looked at me and I gave a smile that said that if he stayed any longer, he would be intruding. So, he made his way inside the house. Then, as he walked inside the house, mama did something that was quite out of the ordinary. Usually, she spoke English to accommodate the guests that didn't speak English and even that was not too often, but when she was alone with her daughters, she would go back to her mother tongue, but this time, she started, "You deserve some explanations, Renee."

I had never heard my mother pronounce my name. Though I was still looking to keep my distance from her, I stayed calm to keep the situation from getting out of control; especially since my mother called me Renee for the first time. I said, "Go ahead."

"I never hated you, *mi hija*. I hated myself . . ."

---

[46] How have you been?

[47] I have had better days. And you?

[48] Same.

She bit her lower lip, waited. Then she took a deep breath and continued, "You know that I was born in Puerto Rico and that my parents died a little while after I was born, right?"

I nodded.

"I was living with my aunt when I met Alejandro. I loved life when I was younger. I loved having fun, like your sister. I didn't love Alejandro, but he studied in America and I wanted to go to that country. I knew that he was in love with me and I told myself that I would learn to love him. He was a good and respectable man. So we got married and then, moved to America. I didn't know much English. All I was learning was on TV, but I learned quick. I loved shows with *Negros* acting in it. I don't know why, but I was attracted. Then, after Maria was born, Leon showed up."

"Mr. Samuels?" I asked.

She nodded, closing her eyes with a smile, enjoying the memory. She then continued, "He was Alejandro's partner . . . So handsome. I loved his eyes. Whenever he came, I would always feel weird around him. A good weird, I mean. I thought I loved Alejandro because he was Maria's father, but I never felt like that with him. It was weird. I tried to think of other things or walk away when he came, but I think I was in love with him already. Then, Ale's mother got sick in Puerto Rico. Ale was given time off by his boss and he told Leon to come by the house to look after us once in a while. That was a mistake.

Leon came the night Ale left. Your sister was sleeping. I brought him in the kitchen because I cooked dinner. He stood a little too close to me. I was able to smell him."

She then looked up and closed her eyes again. The passion she felt for him was palpable. She took a deep breath, and said, "I loved his smell."

Looking at me again, she said, "It drove me crazy!"

With tears in my eyes, I asked, "So you loved Mr. Samuels?"

Mama looked at me, crying and nodded, with a slight smile. I asked, "Why did you stop him from seeing me?"

Mama was still crying when she looked down and said, "I hated myself because I knew Ale killed himself because of us and because of that, I tried to hate Leon."

"Did you try to get an abortion?"

The elderly woman looked at me and I saw pain in her watery eyes. Biting her lower lip again, she looked down again, afraid to answer.

Her reaction, however, answered my question. I was never wanted. Why didn't she go through with it? I looked up to the sky and swallowed whatever saliva was in my mouth as though I was swallowing the outburst of tears that wanted to come out. I always knew that she didn't want me. I knew it, God, I knew it! But it hurt me so much. Why didn't she go through with it?

My voice started breaking as I looked at her and asked, "What is it that changed your mind?"

Usually aware of my surroundings, I had not paid attention to who could come from behind me or walking the streets. All I could do is jump as I heard that voice say, "I told her that enough people had lost their lives."

I turned around and my eyes were fixated on my biological father. He put a hand on my shoulder and smiled at me. He then looked towards mama and made his way towards her. I kept looking at him. As I saw him sitting down next to her and after seeing my mother rest her hand on his lap, like it was the end of a Valentine's Day special on TV. I asked, "Were you waiting for him to come?"

Mama smiled at the gentleman with gentle eyes and said, "I called him here."

Mr. Samuels returned the smile to my mother and then said to me, "Esperanza and I agreed that we had some unfinished business."

"So just like that you guys get back together? I mean, she stops you from seeing me all these years and you are ok with it?"

Embarrassed by my comment, Mama looked down again. The truth was cutting through her. Mr. Samuels took a deep breath and said to me, "Ale's death was a big blow to your mother. She didn't know how to take it. The father of her first child was dead and that was because she was having the baby of his so-called best friend."

Leon did the same as my mother and looked down in shame as well, after saying that, as tears ran down his cheeks. I looked at them both and saw the sadness that situation had created for them. I understood that the situation why they were sad was not because of me, but because they lost a great friend in Alejandro Rodriguez, a man who meant the world to them. But what about me?

"I'm upset cause I was cheated out of everything a girl would've wanted in my life."

Mama said, "*Querida*! What we lost in Ale, you bring it back 300 times more. You are our daughter."

I looked at her coldly and asked, "Where were you when I wanted to hear that? What is it that is making you act this way now? Is it this wheelchair?"

The older woman got up and walked towards me, still crying.

"When you got shot and I thought you were dead, I thought I was going to die!"

She kneeled down, with her hands clasped together and said, "I'm begging you, Renee, please forgive me for being a horrible mother! I'm begging you, *mi hija*!"

Wow, was the first thing that came to mind. Never did I see my mother like that. I was angry. I really was, but right there, in front of me, for the first time, I was going to get the one thing that I always wanted all these years that I lived under her care. I moved forward with my arms opened and embraced her.

CHAPTER 36

Why Me

We walked away from the RIC (Rehabilitation Institute of Chicago), Christopher and I. It was the treatment center that was supposed to help me get back to walking again. Two hours of forcing myself to walk being supported with wooden beams on each side of me, doctors making the necessary tests on my movements and psychiatrists talking to me to make sure that I had not lost my mind. I was already two weeks into the program and I had not lost my mind.

After my session at the RIC, we had decided to go to Southgate Market and just walk around the area. From there, we made our way down South Canal Street. Passing by a few stores with TVs in them, you could still hear the news talking about the earthquake in Haiti a few months prior. Thinking of the devastation, I felt for them, but then again, I had my own problems. As we *walked* (I wished), I saw a *Karl Kani* store and felt the desire to replenish my wardrobe.

"You know what? There's a top that I'd love to go get in that store."

Chris looked at his cell phone and said, "I have a customer who's at a coffee shop in the area, so how about I meet you back here in 1 hour?"

I told him that I needed a top, not the whole store.

"One hour?"

"When you get to shopping, you know how you get. I'm not even trying to come a minute earlier."

I laughed and said, "Yeah, but I know what I'm going to get though."

"Exactly! If you were undecided, I would've said two hours."

We both laughed. Christopher then leaned towards me and kissed me. He then said, "I'll see you later."

I smiled and said, "Later."

I enjoyed the dynamics we possessed, me and him. He was with work a lot, but he made time to hang out with me, even if it meant taking me to the rehab clinic. At times, when work called, on weekends, he'd go running, but he was still coming to me, which I appreciated.

I went into the store and looked around, knowing exactly what I wanted, but still browsing for anything else that could be of interest to me.

"Can I help you with anything?"

A young girl looked at me. She was probably 10 years younger than me. Blonde hair in her, and the way she was dressed, she would have made Britney Spears proud. All Karl Kani merchandise, but it seemed like she decided to put on the underwear only. A top that stopped barely under her breasts and jean shorts that were so tight and short, I knew that if she was bent over, this would mean the end of them.

"No thanks, I'm just browsing."

She smiled and I recognized that smile. It was the same smile I always got when people saw me in the wheel chair. They didn't know me, but they offered their pity. They saw me as weak and helpless.

"Well, tell me if you need anything. My name is Jenny."

I smiled politely and rolled myself to the sweater that I wanted to get quickly. I didn't want to have to deal with that nonsense any longer.

I had spent exactly 15 minutes before being done. I was glad because I was going to prove to Christopher that I didn't need to spend a full hour in the store, which I usually did.

Once I was out of the store, I began making my way down Canal Street, looking in every store around me. As I was about to reach W. Roosevelt Road, I saw Chris from afar on the other side of the street. He was with a white woman there. A potential client, for sure. I knew that it would be unprofessional of me, but I was excited to see him and talk to him.

He had become the ultimate support system, always by my side and taking me to important appointments. So something as frivolous as me not shopping as long as he claimed I would; was just another opportunity to talk to him again.

And so, I started to roll myself to the other side of the street, but then heard a big horn from an oncoming truck. The truck was still a long distance away, so I held each wheels with my hands stopping myself from going any further in between two parked white vans. I then looked at Christopher again and saw him, caught in an embrace with the other woman at the café. I looked and I tried to think that I was seeing things, but he was kissing that woman.

Seeing that, I remembered wondering one time what was the problem with Chris. Simon was the devil incarnate, Richard was a demon and Chris . . . Well, after seeing that, I could only quote the Bible. He came to me in sheep clothing, but inside was a ravenous wolf.

I was tired. I had enough. All the pain, all the suffering . . . What was the point?

And then, it happened. How? I don't know. Maybe I was pushed or maybe I purposely lost my grip on the wheels of my wheelchair. The wind, which had been absent lately in my life, was present that day. Maybe the blame could be put on the wind.

The driver wouldn't get a chance to react in time either. I was in the middle of the road, in the truck's trajectory.

Within two seconds of all that metal making contact with me; just after I was done complaining about all my life and the issue I was going through; the one and only thing thought that came before I came in contact with all that metal was . . .

I want to live.

THE END